Ans	_____	M.L.	_____
ASH	_____	MLW	_____
Bev	_____	Mt.Pl	_____
C.C.	_____	NLM	_____
C.P.	_____	Ott	11/09.
Dick	_____	PC	_____
DRZ	_____	PH	_____
ECH	_____	P.P.	_____
ECS	_____	Pion.P.	_____
Gar	_____	Q.A.	_____
GRM	_____	Riv	_____
GSP	_____	RPP	_____
G.V.	_____	Ross	4/09 McGeein 1969
Har	_____	S.C.	_____
JPCP	_____	St.A.	_____
KEN	_____	St.J	_____
K.L.	_____	St.Joa	_____
K.M.	_____	St.M.	_____
L.H.	_____	Sgt	_____
LO	_____	T.H.	_____
Lyn	_____	TLLO	_____
L.V.	_____	T.M.	_____
McC	_____	T.T.	_____
McG	_____	Ven	_____
McQ	_____	Vets	_____
MIL	_____	VP	_____
	_____	Wat	_____
	_____	Wed	_____
	_____	WIL	_____
	_____	W.L.	_____

FELICITY MOON

When, in self defence, Felicity Moon strikes her employer Julian Cannon, she is forced to leave the place where her father had sent her for her own safety. Accused and jailed for bank-rolling smugglers, Squire Moon is unaware of the dangers Felicity is facing. She is given one last chance by Cannon's housekeeper in the form of a reference to Mr Lucas Packman, a man her father distrusts. Felicity faces a stark choice: trust Packman or her father.

VALERIE HOLMES

FELICITY MOON

Complete and Unabridged

LINFORD
Leicester

First published in Great Britain in 2009

First Linford Edition
published 2009

British Library CIP Data

Holmes, Valerie
　　Felicity Moon.—Large print ed.—
　　Linford romance library
　　1. Love stories
　　2. Large type books
　　I. Title
　　823.9′2 [F]

ISBN 978–1–84782–528–5

Published by
F. A. Thorpe (Publishing)
Anstey, Leicestershire

Set by Words & Graphics Ltd.
Anstey, Leicestershire
Printed and bound in Great Britain by
T. J. International Ltd., Padstow, Cornwall

This book is printed on acid-free paper

1

Felicity Moon was in trouble yet again. This time she had no notion as to how to extricate herself from it. She could hardly deny she had acted improperly, no matter what the provocation. However, she told herself repeatedly that she had a very good reason for her dramatic actions. Usually, she could find a way out of the worst of any situation, but this time it was his word against hers — and he was the master of the house.

Normally, her active mind, charm and, she had to admit, a good share of luck, saved her from further rebukes. Today as she walked the long carpeted corridor towards the polished door in front of her, she could not help feeling as if luck had deserted her. There was no convincing response she could give; no possible defence for her action that would be taken as acceptable by her 'betters' and that meant she, along with her position, was lost.

'Felicity!' Her name resounded down the passage. Even a solid door could not soften the anger emanating from the person within the room. Felicity hesitated, just for a moment — a moment too long, which was not a wise thing to do under the circumstances.

'Felicity Moon!' the voice boomed. She noted that it had risen an octave.

Felicity shook involuntarily. She stretched out her fingers and clenched them into fists by her side, trying to steady her nerves. 'Come on, you can do this, Fliss.' Somehow repeating her father's pet name for her gave her a way to find some comfort and strength from its use. She straightened her apron and skirts and approached the housekeeper's office. Lightly, she tapped on the door and shook her head in annoyance, wishing she had been firmer — making a more decisive sound. If she lay down like a doormat, she knew she could expect to be walked on. Sharply, she took one more large, deep breath, corrected her posture by putting her shoulders back and lifted her chin slightly. She'd fight her corner somehow.

'Enter!' the sharp voice of Miss Edna Richards.

Felicity opened the door and stepped boldly inside; she had intended to force a smile onto her face but as her eyes met the ice-cold stare of Miss Richards', she changed her mind. Instead, whilst adopting a solemn countenance, she restrained her natural instinct to try to make light of the situation after judging the depth of scorn held in her superior's eyes — it was, she realised, a wise decision.

Miss Richards' arms were folded across the rigid bodice of her dress, her features as set in their line as the starched bonnet upon her head. 'You impudent, ungrateful wench! You redefine the term 'dullard'. What in heaven's name — or should I say hell's name, possessed you to do such a thing?' For a moment her expression softened as she looked genuinely bemused at Felicity.

'I . . . ' Felicity began to speak but stopped as soon as Edna stepped in front of her. The woman peered down at her as she continued to release her pent up frustration.

'Have you totally lost leave of your senses? You struck the master!' The woman's eyes appeared to have developed a nervous twitch as she released her tirade upon Felicity, who was fighting hard not to cringe at the force, and truth of every word fired at her.

'He . . . '

'He! He! Do you refer to 'The Master', the owner of this grand house? Listen to the words and take in their meaning, girl! Mister Julian should never be referred to as 'he' by a mere servant girl!'

Felicity tilted her head up slightly and stared defiantly at the older, taller woman. 'The Master,' Felicity stressed the words, 'placed his hand on my buttocks and made an improper suggestion to me. I merely reacted as any decent lady would.' Felicity strongly defended her position — or at least tried to.

' 'Lady', is it?' Miss Richards moved forwards and pointed a finger at Felicity's face. 'You, 'miss', are a servant here. Your education and past might set you apart from the other girls, which is why you were taken on as my assistant in the first place. Do you realise how the master reviles bookish girls? I tried to keep you away from him, but you had to slip into the library and take liberties with his belongings.' Miss Richards shook her head. The lace on her bonnet hardly moved, so efficient was the woman's care of it. 'However, you have gone too far this time — foolish, foolish, girl!'

'He tried to grab me, Miss Richards. What was I supposed to do? It was he who took the liberties!' Felicity did not raise her voice, even though she wanted to shout her words out as loudly as she could. The injustice of it hurt her so much. She stared straight into Miss

Richards' eyes. 'What was I to do
. . . let him have his way?'

The woman turned away from her,
returning to her desk. 'No . . . not at
all, of course not, but you could have
run away and hidden. No, you were
correct to stop him, but you went too
far . . . you struck him. Do you realise
that if he had not been in such high
spirits you could be . . . '

'Drunk, Miss Richards, he was as
drunk as a . . . '

'Mind your language, Felicity! I'll not
have you talking like a ragamuffin, for if
he had so wished you could have been
keeping the company of such in the
local gaol.' Edna sighed, and looked at
her thoughtfully for a moment. 'I took
you in here because I worked for your
father for years and despite everything
that befell him, I . . . '

Felicity stepped forward and leaned
over the desk. 'He was and is an
innocent man!' She defended her father
vehemently, this time it was her anger
mixed with frustration showing.

Miss Richards looked her straight in the eyes. 'You are so like him and that is why for your own protection, and despite my better judgement, I have found you a placement away from here. Not, I may add, at the inn the master recommended to me, but at a place where I think even you would be hard pressed to upset anyone.' Miss Richards lifted a folded piece of paper from the desk and handed it to Felicity. 'This is the address you will travel to.' She picked up letter to a Mr Lucas Packman. 'You will hand this to the doorman and wait until you are seen. Hopefully . . . prayerfully, you will be accepted for a position that I had even considered filling myself. Do not make a fool of yourself or discredit my good name, Felicity. This may well be your only chance, to have a respectable life. Your father is in no position to help you and his relatives have made it quite clear they do not wish to be associated with him or his offspring.' She folded her arms.

Felicity looked down thoughtfully at the two pieces of paper she held in her hand. She felt moved in an unusual way. Looking at Edna's face — Miss Richards, to everyone else in the house — she was filled with sadness. 'Who is he?'

'Your new master! One who will be able to keep you in service and in line, I hope. He is not a drinking man, nor is he given to . . . to taking advantage of young women. However, neither will he stand for anything less than total loyalty and good service.'

Felicity listened to the woman's words and let her anger disperse. 'I'm sorry, I let you down,' she said softly. 'Edna . . . '

Edna placed her hand gently on Felicity's. 'No, lass, you let yourself down. Don't do it again. Time is not on your side. You have to find a safe and stable home because if you don't and your father's predicament becomes known, no one will want you in their service. They just wouldn't trust the daughter of a . . . ' Edna looked away. 'You have already lost your rank in society and your home, don't lose everything else. Try to maintain at least some respect and honour.'

'And will this be that, Miss Richards, a safe home?' Felicity held up the address. The brief moment of intimacy had passed and they were back to their formal positions in life.

'I wish I knew for sure, Felicity, but the truth is I know of no other option that is suitable. This reference is from me, not the master. It will do for Mr Packman, but would not be even considered by respectable people.'

'Respectable people should not prey on undefended servants!' Felicity answered sharply.

'Silence, Miss Moon!' Miss Richards rebuked her quietly withdrawing her hand.

'Do you know this man Mr Packman?' Felicity looked at the lady whom she had worked for these past six months, but the way her head turned to other matters laid upon the desk told Felicity that she would not receive an answer to this important question. It appeared her future would have to be based on how much she trusted this woman's judgement.

There was a knock on the door. 'Come in.' Miss Richards spoke loudly as if she was glad of the interruption.

'Jacob said the cart will be ready to take Moon to town in an hour, ma'am,' the maid announced.

'Thank you, Annie.' Without looking at Felicity again she merely said, 'Leave your uniform on your bed. You just pack up your belongings and be gone before the master awakes.'

There was nothing more left to say or do. Felicity ignored the satisfied look on the maid's face. The girl had taken an instant dislike to Felicity the moment she had arrived at the house.

'Come in, Annie. We have work to do now.' Edna's voice sounded resigned to the decisions she had made.

'Yes, Miss Richards, you can depend

on me.' The door was shut firmly behind her and Felicity was left in the corridor. She glanced down at her hands and gritted her teeth. Whoever Mr Packman was she did not know, but it appeared her future at least for now lay with him.

Felicity ran back to her room comforted by the knowledge that she did not have to see 'The Master' again.

2

Two hours later Felicity was sitting precariously on a fence waiting for the coach to arrive. She had been there for what seemed an age, her coat barely keeping her warm. The coach was late. The journey from the hall to this point had been bumpy and uncomfortable, but the driver had said the coach would arrive soon, and then he had left her. But how soon was soon? What if it wasn't going to come at all? Would she be abandoned there for the night? She shivered at such a frightening proposition. The sky was already becoming dusky and the temperature cooler as an icy wind gathered strength.

Staring at the letter addressed to Mr Lucas Packman, she wondered if she dared to open it. What did it say? Who or what was this man? Why should he accept her on the words of Miss

Richards alone? So many questions ran through her mind, but no answers followed them. Felicity wondered what would have happened if she had not slapped Mr Julian Cannon. Would he have left her alone if she had asked him politely to take his hand from her person? She shook her head, accepting that she would never know the answer as she had reacted on instinct, choosing her path of action, which had determined her current fate.

Her finger played with the edge of the folded paper, sliding underneath the neatly tied blue ribbon. Perhaps if she was careful, no one would know that she had opened it and peeped inside. After all, it was written about her. Would it say why she had left her last place of employment? She was about to try to slip the letter free of its tethers when the sound of a horse's hooves made her lose her nerve and she slipped the letter back into her pocket. Guiltily, she looked up and stood next to her bag.

Felicity was filled with apprehension as there was no coach in sight, only a solitary figure driving a fashionable gig. The vehicle stopped some three feet from her. A tall figure, wearing a large overcoat and wide-brimmed hat climbed down. The man had the stance and gait of a gentleman; confident and strong.

'Miss, do you await the coach to Selby?' he asked as he neared her.

'Yes, sir,' she answered, trying to sound confident and not the least bit afraid of the handsome stranger.

'Then you are in for an extremely long wait. Unfortunately, the horse stumbled and has caused an accident. It shall be some time before the vehicle will be righted. In fact, I know that it shall not be along today.' He stood before her, and without further explanation bent down and picked up her bag. 'You'll have to come with me, Miss Moon.'

'Sir!' she spoke out, rather louder than she had expected to.

He stopped, momentarily, glancing down at her.

'Who are you?'

He placed the bag down on the ground once more and faced her. 'I apologise, miss. However, I am being abrupt because I travel in haste. I have been requested to collect you and escort you to your destination, which is Marram Hall I believe, if you are Miss Felicity Moon. I am late, and therefore anxious to be on my way. Could we continue now, please?' He gestured to the gig.

'But who are you, sir? I can hardly travel with someone who has no name and how do you know mine and where it is I am destined to go?' Felicity followed him as he continued toward the vehicle.

'I am tired, ma'am. This is not the way I choose to make introductions to young ladies. Miss Richards, Edna, my old governess, sent word you were to arrive today and requested that I meet your coach. However, a traveller told me of the coach's predicament and I have ventured miles out of my way in order to reach here. If you will climb up we may return to the hall before dark. Otherwise, we should be forced to rent rooms at an inn which I would find highly objectionable.' His stern expression did nothing to put Felicity at ease. She did not know whether to take offence at his words and attitude.

'Not that your company would not be pleasant enough, just I have no wish to sleep in some flea infested bed. Neither do I wish to become fodder for highwaymen and rogues on the open road. You can call me 'sir', or Mr Packman, until we are better acquainted in my home. I am Lucas Packman, and therefore possibly your new employer, Miss Moon. Now, please . . . can we continue?' He held out a hand toward the open road.

'Yes, thank you.' Felicity seated herself next to him, thinking what a strange man Miss Richards had sent her to. She had barely sat down when the gig was moved forward. She was not used to being so high and held on firmly the side as the vehicle jolted along the newly covered road. It was far smoother than the old weather worn tracks.

'Hold on tightly, for I do not intend to idle.' He looked at her, before flicking the reins at the horse's rear. 'I hope you are not of faint heart, miss.'

'I never have been, sir,' she answered politely, and saw a grin cross his face.

'Good.' He increased the pace. They moved forward swiftly and at first Felicity was shaken by the speed, but then as the wind refreshed her face she started to enjoy the exhilarating feeling. This journey was far more exciting than the slow plod of the cart.

They travelled in silence for some miles, but inevitably the weather closed in and, as the day darkened, the clouds that had dogged their path began to shed their rain.

Somewhat reluctantly, he manoeuvred the gig into the yard of an inn.

They were cold, wet and tired.

Lucas jumped down and a boy ran out of the stables and took the reins from him. He tossed the boy a coin and said, 'Bring the bag inside.' Without hesitation he came to Felicity's side as she was trying to find the wet step to climb down. She felt his hands upon her waist as bodily she was lifted and swung around to the shelter of the porch of the inn. There, her feet found solid ground once more.

'It would appear we are to stay at one of these infernal places after all.' Releasing her, he entered the inn. The threshold was worn down by many a traveller's footsteps, and wet. She hesitated at the noise and smells from within. People stared at her as she stood in the doorway to what seemed a small open room with settles either side of a warm flickering fire. He walked over to the men sitting by the hearth and spoke quietly to them, again flicking them a coin. They vacated their seats and pulled up three legged stools at a table by the window, continuing to smoke their clay pipes and eagerly ordering more ale. One seemed to be in what had been the well-fitted red jacket of a possibly once proud soldier. Now both the wearer and the cloth looked somewhat dog-eared and faded.

Lucas Packman glanced around. Seeing Felicity was completely lost in this masculine world, he took her by the hand and brought her to the settle, placing her nearest the fire.

'Do not worry, miss. I shall insist upon clean bedding. My hatred of inns is a view peculiar to myself and my own standards. Do not worry yourself over my rash comments earlier. It is better that we rest here in the warmth than soak ourselves to the skin,' he looked at her slightly impishly after the openness of his words. Such mention of anything to do with the natural state of the body would be highly unacceptable in polite society, but he appeared to be appraising her reaction and dismissed such fanciful notions, returning to practical speech, he continued, 'drenched by the elements.' He smiled at her as if to reassure Felicity that all would be well, but she sensed his unease.

Felicity was not sure if his words were sincere, but she nodded as if in acceptance of them.

'Two jugs of ale, and a plate of your finest cut of meat and vegetables.' He spoke to a thin girl who served the drinks. She bobbed a little curtsey and, Felicity thought she saw her flicker her eyelashes a little oddly at him.

'Yes, sir.'

Felicity watched him.

'Have you a room available here tonight?' he asked the girl unenthusiastically.

'There be beds for use in the loft, sir. Fresh straw and blankets changed at the end every week,' she added proudly, and smiled at him. They can be real cosy.

'Let me see what is available.' He patted Felicity's knee. She glared at his familiar manner but if he noticed he did not show it. 'I will only be gone a few moments, warm yourself here and do not worry. I shall return in a moment.'

He left her and she saw him climb a narrow ladder into the loft space of the inn. In less than a couple of moments he returned, rather swiftly brushing the sleeves of his coat as if he found the dust offensive. He called to a man in the back room.

Felicity couldn't be sure if anyone had heard him for the men in the room were laughing loudly. She dare not look at them in case it was her presence that was causing them to behave so. She could just make out the outline of Lucas exchange something from his pocket to the stout man wearing a grubby apron who stood in the doorway. Both men disappeared from view as they walked down an adjacent corridor.

After a few moments, Lucas Packman returned and smiled at her. 'We are sorted, ma'am,' he said brightly.

She noticed he had not used her name. Then he looked at the young woman who served the drinks. 'Bring our food to our room when it is ready. Come with me,' he held a hand out to her and as soon as she was within reach cupped her elbow, 'Don't worry, we shall be dry and moderately comfortable tonight. We shall continue our journey tomorrow and then I shall see if you are suitable for the position as offered.'

Felicity was about to ask what the position was, when she was handed an oil lamp and led down a long corridor to a room at the rear of the inn. The passage ended in a small staircase which opened onto a bed chamber. She was faced with a double four-posted bed, a table and chair within it. The fire flickered in the hearth, filling the low beamed room with a warm glow.

Her bag had been placed at the end of the bed. 'I shall give you some moments to change into your dry night attire, whilst I have a drink of porter and warm myself by the inn's fire. I shall return shortly; we are in luck as this room was prepared for a Lady. However, she was on the upturned coach and has had to take lodgings elsewhere. We shall rest well tonight and be fresh for our journey the morrow.' He turned to leave her.

'Mr Packman, is this a jest? You expect me to change into my night clothes here, sir?' Felicity asked in disbelief as she felt the warm air from the fire upon her cheeks, and smelt the moisture rise from her soaked skirts.

'In preference to contracting a bout of pneumonia, my advice would be ... yes, and quite soon. What would you suggest you do? Spending a night in the chair draped with sodden garments would hardly be commodious to either of us.' He looked at her and shrugged at her defiant stance. 'Miss, I have no patience with false modesty. In my chosen employment I see all kinds of humanity displayed before me. I do not aim to see your anatomy in detail which is why I shall remove myself for some moments. Please, change out of that attire, you are wet. Dry yourself quickly, spread your clothes near the fire and allow us to have some food and rest.' He left the room without waiting for, or apparently wanting a reply. Felicity stood askance at his attitude.

More questions returned to her — what employment was he in? What on earth was the position she had been sent to fill? What would Miss Richards expect her to do under the circumstance? An image of her father crossed her mind, but she dismissed it in an instance. This arrangement would be seen as her ruin, yet, soaking wet, cold and tired, it seemed the only practical course of action to take. Felicity removed her soaked skirt.

3

Felicity removed the rest of her wet clothes and quickly changed into her dry undergarments, pulling a nightdress over her head and wrapping a blanket around herself as a shawl. She had thought of exchanging her damp clothes for her good dress, refusing to let him see her in her nightdress. However, her 'good' dress was also the only other one she carried with her, and she had no wish to crease it so soon into her new start in life. If she had to leave this arrogant man and make her own way she would need to make a good impression in order to find herself another position in a respectable household. The thought frightened her because she had no references bar the one addressed to Mr Lucas. She felt trapped. Deciding she had at least tried to preserve her modesty, if not ruined her reputation, she set to brushing out her long dark damp hair and tried to dry it in front of the open fire. This seemed a luxury when good firewood was in such short supply. The wars with France had been a huge drain on all the country's resources, not just on the many men needed to fight Napoleon's war machine.

Her thoughts were interrupted when Felicity heard more people arrive at the inn, rather noisily. Boisterous voices drifted along the narrow corridor, sounding almost as though they were approaching the door to the bedchamber. Felicity knew this would not be so, as she could hear them ordering jugs of porter, but the voices were very strange and disturbing to her, coupled with the fact that she found herself sharing a room with Miss Richards' friend. How she missed her home. There she had had maids of her own, a room for her clothes and the freedom of her father's small but prosperous estate. There she had known what freedom was. She stepped back as a piece of firewood fell into the hearth, spluttering before the flame died out. Despite the sadness that filled her for her lost past, she vowed that she would not let her own spark die. Somehow she would rescue her father and return him to that estate. It was a home she had loved so dearly.

She could see an upside down image of the door to the room from where she hung her head. She stared at it anxiously, brushing out her hair whilst drying her locks, when it opened wide and Lucas Packman appeared in the doorway. Quickly she stood upright flicking her thick dark hair back over her shoulders.

He paused for a moment before entering the room and stared at her silently.

'You were swift, sir,' Felicity commented, as she tied her unruly hair back with her ribbon.

'The room became crowded with wet, cold travellers. I decided to vacate it and let them benefit from the fire, as we have one of our own. He entered the bedchamber closing the door behind him, turning the key within the lock. He had brought in with him a tray on which their supper plates had been placed. 'Our food is basic, but appears to be quite fresh.'

He placed the tray on the table and then raised his gaze to stare into her eyes and smiled. 'Miss Moon, allow me to introduce myself properly. My name is Lucas Packman. I am a surgeon. My line of work affords me a directness regarding the human anatomy, which may sometimes appear to leave me short of manners when dealing with young ladies. May I offer my sincere apologies?' He bowed his head slightly in what appeared to be a small gesture of humility. It was one which Felicity thought was an effort to him, a somewhat unfamiliar one to this proud and distinguished man.

'Thank you, sir. I accept them and would add that I did not know who or what you were. Neither do I have any notion as to the position I am applying for.' She was standing with her back to the warmth of the fire and thought she saw a flicker of amusement in his eyes. 'I should never have entertained the notion of staying in such a place with a stranger if you had not been highly regarded by my good friend, Miss Edna Richards.' Her cheeks were flushed deeper but she held her head high.

'Then let us take this time together to familiarise ourselves with each other and discover if we are truly compatible as people, for we shall be spending a lot of time in each other's company.' He sat on the chair next to the table, but as Felicity held firm to the shawl gathered around her, raising an eyebrow at him, he openly laughed at her.

'Relax, Miss Moon, I merely mean we should eat and talk. Discuss matters. Then sleep and make our way tomorrow to Marram Hall. We shall make a fresh start. Do not paint me as a monster of the night who absconds with an innocent young girl to incarcerate her in the bowels of an inn. There is too much of a trend for this fantastic nonsense. The Phantasms of novellas may corrupt an innocent mind, terrifying young maids by feeding them wild ideas. However, you are intelligent so do not fall into this type of foolishness.'

'I am not so easily influenced by such 'novellas'. I use my common sense, sir.' Felicity's anger was rising. She was tired in body and of this uncertainty. If she had to, she would defend herself in any way necessary.

'And what is your 'common sense' telling you now, Felicity?' He looked at her as if trying to appraise her thoughts.

'It tells me that I am locked into a room, with a stranger who purports to be a surgeon and who has taken control of my life. As I said, if it was not that you came to me recommended by Miss Richards I would not even entertain the idea of staying here!' Felicity had tried not to raise her voice. However, she had been angered at his suggestion that she was some sort of feeble, impressionable mind.

He sighed and stared directly at her. 'You are well educated, Felicity. I apologise again if I offered you offence. I fear I have kept the company of books for too long. I need a strong minded woman, who will not faint at the sight of blood. Who can come somewhere near a match to my intellect and who can share a vision.' He walked over to her. 'I need someone whom I can trust — who in turn will trust me. You are showing you have intelligence, but I need more than that — I need a housekeeper, an assistant and a companion. Edna has turned my offer aside and has sent you in her place. Why, I am not certain. She and I have always been on good terms. You are certainly more attractive and younger than Edna, but these were aspects I put aside in preference for the afore mentioned qualities. She follows my ideals and has shown excellent skills in her work. I can only assume that you have impressed her greatly. However, I presumed she would have discussed the matter with you in depth. If you are in such ignorance of this state of affairs then may I ask, why? Did you leave your last establishment in haste?' He was watching her closely.

Felicity swallowed and remembered the letter Miss Richards had given her and felt her cheeks burn. She had been so caught up in the unfolding events that she had not given it a thought. Felicity quickly retrieved it from her bag and handed it to Lucas. He gestured to her that she should eat as he read Edna's message.

She could not bring herself to eat. What if the note told him of her circumstances? What would he think of her then? Yet he said he needed someone whom he could trust and vice-versa.

'So tell me of the circumstances of your departure.' He was watching and assessing her reply.

Felicity took in a deep breath, braced

herself and confessed, 'I struck the master of the house because he made an improper gesture toward me.' She then added boldly, 'and I should not hesitate to do the same again, should such a circumstance present itself.'

He grinned at her. 'I have been duly warned.' His next question took her by surprise and her confidence visibly waned. 'Who was your father, Miss Moon?'

'A good man,' she replied, her voice lowered as did her eyes.

'I asked who he was, not what?' he replied calmly.

'A squire and a good man who helped his tenants. He actively tried to improve their lot in life throughout such hard times.' She stared at him, feeling the tension rise inside her. She was at this man's mercy. He was a man of position and she the daughter of a man in gaol.

'Where is he now?' he persisted.

'In gaol, accused of giving money to smugglers to buy contraband,' she looked at the fire momentarily, 'but he is innocent!' she declared, with as much passion in her voice and eyes as the heat of the flames that reached out into the air. 'He would never help those people. Smugglers are no less than thieves, some even murder. They fund Napoleon's war!' She looked up at him almost pleading with him to believe her words. 'He is innocent — smugglers give Napoleon the coin he needs to defeat our own army!'

'So you understand enough of politics to see that the 'free trade' supplies our enemies with English gold to prop up the Franc. I am impressed; most just see a quick profit. I have no knowledge of your father, his character or circumstances, but I admire your honesty and your directness. Now, if you will allow me I shall explain to you what I am about and you can decide if you wish to take the position. I shall then sleep atop the covers and you shall sleep soundly and safely beneath them.' He placed the note onto the table and offered her a plate of food. 'Eat now, please.'

Felicity took it gratefully, relieved by his words, but realised that the note had been short. Edna had not revealed anything of her past, or her father's situation, so Felicity had no need to confess any of it. She bit into a piece of cheese and sipped a glass of Normandy wine, but inside she felt a sense of relief. She was glad that she had spoken out, for in truth there was a sense of freedom in it, and for her father there would have to be again or he would die in gaol.

* * *

They ate in silence. He appeared to be mulling over the information he had just learned.

'I live in a lonely house on the northeast coast. It is a beautiful, wild place, but it does not lend itself to fashion, society or luxury. I have purchased it to turn it into a hospital. I am tired of the rules of ignorant governors and of the influence of politics in the city. I wish to take my learning further and help those who have been considered by my fellow surgeons to be beyond care. This means that I shall accept some paying patients, but hope also to help those in the community who can ill afford to pay for treatment, yet who might be able to help the hall with their produce or labour. In time, I may be able to employ other staff, but to start with I will train my own nurses and helpers, and I need a person to help administer the hall and be my personal assistant. Does this sound at all conducive to you?'

He looked at her and she noticed that his deep brown eyes were far more astute than they had at first appeared. She had assumed he was pre-occupied with his own thoughts and plans but he had been appraising her from the very first moment of their meeting. He was a man who understood people.

'You would still consider me for the position after I told you my father is in gaol?' She stood before him feeling more vulnerable than she had with Cannon. He had seen her as a servant he had purchased; what she was asking of Mr Packman was to accept her for the person she truly was.

'Yes, because you are honest and I admire that quality in a human above all else. I also do not judge the child by the parent's deeds . . . or their misdeeds.' He yawned. 'Excuse me. It has been a very long day.'

'Then I thank you for that because I am not ashamed of my father, he is innocent. Indeed, I am interested. Your idea sounds fascinating. I think you have a noble aim that will be a challenge to put into practice. Sir, are your ideas radical? Do they go outside the established thinking on medicine?' Felicity asked, realising that, if they were, he could be an educated man who was a pioneer in his own right, or possibly a charlatan, a man who wanted to act beyond the moral guidelines of his profession — to play at being God.

'No, miss. I am no radical — I would just have my hospital clean with emphasis on the aftercare, in particular the food fed to the patients as they recover. These are areas which I feel are sadly neglected. Now, I am very tired and I shall talk to you in more detail as we travel tomorrow.'

He stood up and was almost touching her, as his body was so close to hers. Lucas looked down at her face. 'Miss Moon, if you should like to make yourself comfortable in the bed, I should very much like to lie down upon it.' Casually he removed his coat.

'Yes, of course. However, I shall ask you to please not think ill of me if I suggest you remove your wet garments and wrap yourself in this.' She held out the blanket to him and blushed slightly at the familiarity of the gesture.

'Indeed, I would think it a very generous and practical solution. Per-haps, spoken like a nurse, even.' He smiled at her and she climbed into the bed, closed her eyes and was aware that a few short moments later there was a body lying near hers. She felt the warmth and presence of Lucas although their bodies did not touch. Felicity slept despite the noise from the inn, knowing that tomorrow would be the start of, not only a new day, but a whole new way of life.

4

Felicity was pleased on waking to see that a tray had been left by the bed and Lucas Packman had already risen and left the room. She dressed quickly and ate her fill before venturing outside.

The sun shone brightly even though it held no warmth to greet the day. It was very cold, a frosty mist hung over the open moor. Their journey was to start early. She saw Lucas talking to a coachman by the gatepost. He looked ill at ease until he saw her watching him, then he seemed to relax as he stood tall and greeted her.

'I had hoped that I should not need to wake you.' He looked over to where the gig was made ready and the horse, already harnessed waited patiently.

'Shall we go then?' Felicity replied, and stepped towards the patient animal. She was anxious to get away. As she had passed the people of the inn, the looks they had cast her made her feel guilty, yet she had not behaved improperly. Felicity knew from their expressions they had judged her to be a fallen woman. If she was living as part of a respectable family and had any hope of being matched to a suitor, her reputation would have been irreparably damaged. In truth, she had none to consider. Her father had already been ill-judged, so why should she care what strangers thought she was about? However, she did deeply, and therefore she could not wait to leave the place and the feeling of shame behind her.

'Why do you look so serious this morning, Miss Moon? Are you having second thoughts about our arrangements?' Lucas asked her, as he helped her up into the vehicle.

'No. I'm satisfied that the future holds a lot of promise; more so than the present.' She smiled at him a little nervously, aware of his touch and that their every move was being scrutinised.

Her reply was swift but she could not help but glance back over at the innkeeper who was watching them from the inn's door. The driver was leaning on the dry-stone wall near him. Both were grinning as if they shared a private joke at her expense.

'Ignore them, Felicity. They are of simple minds. They do not know what or who you are. Nor what we did or did not do in the room last night, so let them fill their lives with the darker thoughts of their imagination, it is of no import to us.' He climbed up next to her and took the reins. 'They judge yet they do not know the people we are. We do. Or soon will. So hold your head high and be glad you have a safe home to go to, a future to aspire to, and your honour very much intact.' He flicked the reins and they moved off onto the open road.

She looked at his face; it showed confidence and was even slightly defiant. He had dealt with the matter and as far as Lucas Packman was concerned, Felicity thought, to him it appeared that was an end to it.

'Your reputation could be tarnished, sir,' she said simply as they left the inn behind them.

'If it is, then I'm sure I can bear it. Now, do not dwell on what has already been done, it is a waste of energy and time.' He did not take his eyes from the road ahead.

They approached the narrow bridge south of a market town called Gorebeck. Tall new houses had been built to line the road. The stone walkway had two steps to the muddy road making it easy to mount or dismount from horse and carriage alike. But it was not the new, fashionable habitat that took Felicity's attention, rather the auspicious building that appeared at the other side of the bridge, appearing and disappearing through the trees as they travelled. It was set back in its own land, looking stark and impenetrable. Felicity grabbed the seat. Her eyes fixed on the old grey building with its iron barred windows and hidden secrets.

'Is that the gaol?' Felicity asked as the gig was slowed down on the approach to the bridge. The river flowed quite quickly beneath, but its natural beauty was not even noticed by Felicity.

'No, Miss Moon. The prison and court offices are at the opposite end of town. That great monstrosity of a building is the asylum. Believe me, Felicity, it looks far worse from the outside than it does from within.'

'I find that hard to believe.' Felicity stared at it and held tightly to the gig.

'People are ignorant of the work that is being carried out within its gaunt façade, so again their imagination and tongues take flight. It was a place to be feared, I know it, but that has all changed now and a man with a forward thinking mind has taken it over. He works wonders, repairing people's minds and lives. I have visited it several times over the last two years and it is vastly improved. I shall take you there one day.'

Felicity's head spun around not hiding the fear she felt at the thought of going into such a place. She stared at him.

Lucas shook his head and looked back at her. 'You shall have to learn to trust my judgement. I would not take you into anywhere that was ill befitting a young lady's presence,' he explained.

'Some would consider the inn to be such a place,' Felicity answered in a quiet voice.

'Some should mind their own business then. Besides, sometimes necessity dictates we do things outside what is normally accepted as proper. I do not have any patience for this fashion of perfectly healthy people pretending to suffer palpitations at the mere mention of a part of the body. We all share two basic forms of anatomy and neither form should be shrouded in vanity or shame because of 'fashion'.'

She stared at him, admiring his forthrightness. It was he who looked slightly embarrassed at his own outburst, and he swiftly changed the conversation.

'Now you tell me something, Miss Moon, is this where your father is?'

As the gig entered the town, Felicity felt a lump form in her throat. She was so near to her father whom she hadn't seen for nearly six months, yet she was frightened. He could be ill, feeble, or worse, broken in spirit. She wondered if she should pass by. Would Mr Packman give her the time to make a visit? Should she demand that he did? Or, should she go by rather than upset herself and her father. He was a proud man; it could destroy him if she saw him so low.

'Yes,' she said simply not knowing what else to add except, 'He is innocent of the crime.'

'So you say. We shall go via the gaol, but first we need to eat and you may purchase some food in order to present him with a parcel to ease what will be a monotonous diet, I'm sure.' The gig was stopped by a stables and Lucas dismounted making arrangements for his horse to be fed, watered, rested and tended to whilst they went about their business. Felicity should have never doubted him. He, Lucas Packman, had decided her next action for her. He had done what it appeared he was used to and taken charge of the situation. This was obvious, to Felicity, to be an essential part of the man's basic character. He saw no problem as insurmountable; nothing other than a challenge to overcome or work around. The decision was made. He would take her to see her father. Lucas lifted her down from the gig and walked with her to a coffee house.

'Mr Packman,' Felicity began, 'I have no knowledge of how he fares. I have not had word from him for nearly four months . . . he may be ill.' She looked away quickly as she had no wish to make an emotional spectre of herself in front of him. For he was strong and she was equally a match for him in spirit, but this was so much a sensitive matter to her that she did not feel her usual strength.

To her surprise he placed a confident hand upon her shoulder. 'Then, you will be visiting him with the best possible chaperone.'

She looked up at him, his eyes showing an understanding that his actions and manners often appeared to shield. She nodded at him agreeing that fate had possibly blessed her with someone who may yet be able to help her father's plight; she held her head up and smiled at him. 'Yes, of course, you are quite correct. I worry unnecessarily.'

He squeezed her shoulder slightly before letting his hand slip to her elbow, and guided her inside the bay-fronted building where the smell of freshly baked pies greeted them, mingled with the aroma of brewing coffee.

'No, Felicity, you worry not unnecessarily, but like any caring daughter would,' he added, and seated her at a settle in the bay of the window. 'Now, relax. We shall deal with your father's situation afterwards; until then we can do nothing. Therefore be warm and enjoy your food.'

Felicity found his company easy. He told her in more detail of his plans for the hospital and how he expected to fund it. She watched as his voice and manner became more animated, the passion he felt for his work showing in his eyes. He had a manner that was stiff and proper but she could see there was a soul burning within. He stopped suddenly, and looked out of the window. Felicity saw his cheeks flush slightly and realised he had let her see more of his true character than he felt comfortable with. 'We must make haste if we are to fit in a visit to your father. You find the bakers whilst I retrieve the gig.' He stood up and held his hand out for her; their conversation had ended.

If Felicity thought the asylum looked glum from the outside it was nothing to what she was faced with as they approached the gaol. Soldiers were based in the barracks. Once they passed beyond these they were faced with a courtyard with buildings on three sides. To the left was the gaol building. This was obvious from the noises emanating from the high, thick walled façade. What windows there were, were high up and had heavy iron bars adorning them. One double reinforced door was guarded by two red-jacketed soldiers carrying muskets. This was the only perceivable entrance.

In front of them was a newer building with fanlight windows above the central door, and an even pattern of rectangular windows across the two story front. This painted building looked as though it belonged in a different world to the old gaol. A set of carved stone stairs led up to the large, black painted doors at the centre of the building.

To their right was a similarly built, but far less grand building which, from the number of soldiers who came and went through one of its two doors, appeared to be the men's barracks.

Felicity swallowed as the gig was brought to a halt outside the gaol's dominant frontage. A soldier came forward and greeted them.

Lucas jumped down and approached the man. 'Can we see your duty officer, please? I am a surgeon from the Royal College of Edinburgh and I have been asked on behalf of the family of one of your inmates to check his state of health and administer to his needs, should that state require it.'

Felicity watched as he stood tall and delivered this address without hesitation. His confidence and authority were totally convincing in their deliverance.

'If you comes with me I shall see if the sergeant in charge is free to see you, sir.' The soldier glanced back to Felicity. 'Who is she?'

'The lady is my assistant.' Lucas turned to her and winked as he offered her a hand to steady herself as she stepped down from the gig. 'She will accompany me.'

Felicity lifted the parcel of food from the gig and held it protectively in front of her. Lucas had a leather bag in his other hand. He looked at the soldier and asked politely, 'Should we go inside?' as he gestured towards the door of the gaol.

They stepped inside and Felicity let out a little gasp, the place smelt. She was not sure of what, but it was not of anything she had been used to in the hall. The offices were to the right and left of the main entrance. Beyond this entrance hall was a flight of circular iron stairs spiralling down to a stony underground system of rooms. That, she presumed, was where some of the cells were.

'Wait here,' the soldier ordered, and left them sitting on a bench outside one of the offices. She could smell cigar smoke and heard laughter from within. The soldier disappeared inside the room, and the door was shut firmly behind him.

'Why did you not say who I was?

Wouldn't it have been easier to explain the truth of why I am here?' Felicity asked, as Lucas who stood by her, his hands held behind his back, stared around the barren hall.

'Yes, possibly, but that may not have been sufficient to gain access to your father. This way they deal with someone of authority who may have influence with higher ranks than themselves.' He looked down at her. 'It may not be the most straightforward approach, but in this world you have to make your way the best you can. Besides, I may have hidden or stretched the truth but I do not believe I have actually lied.'

'They stared at the door as a voice was raised from within. As the noise echoed off the cold stone walls, Felicity remembered another corridor and another voice booming out at her. Was that all such a short time ago? Yet here she was on the verge of seeing her poor father and with a man she hardly knew who she had shared a night with in a highway inn.

The door opened and the flustered soldier stepped out. 'Pardon, sir,' he asked, 'who is the prisoner that you have come to see?'

Felicity opened her mouth to speak but was surprised when Lucas spoke out her father's name.

'Josiah E. Moon. Now, will this take long? We have a journey to complete.' He looked sternly at the man who took one step back towards the door.

'One more moment, sir.' He ventured inside again.

'How do you know my father's name?' she asked quietly. He either did not hear her or ignored her question, as he gave no response.

In no time a rotund figure wearing sergeant's stripes emerged from the office. His smile was broad and he held outstretched hands to greet Lucas.

'My dear sir, apologies for your time being wasted by this buffoon. Please come with me and you can see Squire Moon immediately. Are you sure you wish this slip of a lass to enter the prison?' He looked Felicity up and down. She was aware that her apprehension at seeing her father again, and not knowing what sight would greet her, could be misconstrued as fear of the place itself.

'I assure you this 'slip of a lady' is more than up to visiting a poor internee.' Lucas was surprised when the man laughed at his words.

'Well, as it is Squire Moon, I suppose I see no harm in it, but I would not let her into the cells.'

Felicity did not like the man's manner. He was, she thought, acting out of character. She doubted he was normally so jocular in his manner but he wanted to impress Lucas, so she followed on behind bracing herself at the thought of going down the dark spiral stairs to the cells below. She had not understood the man's remark. For where else would her father be but in one of them?

5

Instead of leading them down the steps to the lower cells he took them through his office, out into another hallway, which itself led on to another flight of stairs. He did not seem at all bothered by their sudden appearance and Lucas' request to inspect an internee. Their way was made clear by the natural light from small windows. They continued to a door on the first landing. It had a lock, but no more than a normal key had been left in it.

The door was opened wide by the man and then he stepped back allowing Lucas to go inside the room; Felicity was careful to stay immediately behind him. The door was no more than a few inches thick, and of normal width. Light filtered into the room via a high fan window which looked out over the square. The stone floor was covered in three places by clip rugs, one at the side of a well made up bed. The sheets looked clean as did the blankets atop them. A jug and pewter cup were placed on a small table at the side. Sitting in front of a small fire on a moderately comfortable chair was a tall man, with a healthy glow to his cheeks.

'I'll leave you to get acquainted,' the sergeant said, and closed the door behind them.

It was only as Josiah Moon stood to his full height, swapping his pipe to his left hand, and offering his right to shake Lucas' that the man noticed a shocked looking Felicity standing speechless behind him.

'Felicity! What in heaven's name are you doing in a place like this?' His face was stern. He had obviously been caught unexpectedly by her arrival.

Felicity almost moved in slow motion as she stared at the state of her father. His clothes looked laundered and they were his own, as she would expect him to wear at home. He looked well fed, and stood straight as always. No chains adorned these walls which she was grateful for, but he had pen and ink and paper next to him at the fireside table. This was more like a room at an inn than a prison cell.

'Oh, Father!' she exclaimed, flooded with relief that he was well.

'Come here, lass, and give your father a hug.' His voice was smooth as always. He wrapped his arms around her and hugged her to him momentarily. She did not see the cutting look he fixed on Mr Packman.

'Why have you brought my daughter here? Is it not enough that I am in such a place without letting her witness my incarceration first hand?' He released Felicity.

'It was her wish, as she was so concerned for your wellbeing,' Lucas explained and glanced around the room as if surveying the furnishings and warm fire with wonder.

'I brought you some food, Father.' Felicity looked around and saw the remnants of his last meal on a pewter plate left on a low table by the door.

He chuckled and took the bundle from her. 'Indeed you have.' He stared at the pies and smiled. 'Fresh made, too!'

'Your daughter was worried that you may be wasting away or being ill-treated by the soldiers,' Lucas said and seated himself on the bed, placing his bag by his feet.

Squire Moon watched Felicity and shook his head. 'You worry so, just like your mother did before you. I am well able to look after myself. Now explain, girl, how it is you can purchase the services of a doctor to effect your entrance to me? I left you in the care of a good friend; did you have Julian's permission to come here?'

'A surgeon, sir, not a doctor,' Lucas corrected.

Felicity shifted nervously. 'Father, how do you manage to live so well? I am pleased you are here, and not in the cells. Does this mean they know you are innocent and are having the conviction squashed?' She hoped to change the subject and avert his attention from her circumstance. 'You did not write to me. I was so worried about you.'

'Felicity, my news is extremely limited. No, I am still serving my term, but as I am a man with some influence and wealth I have made an arrangement that allows me to do so in some modicum of comfort. I am appealing against the conviction.' He sat back down and stared at Lucas who seemed unimpressed with what he was hearing.

Felicity could feel a growing tension in the air between them. 'Mr Packman kindly agreed to make this visit and put my mind at rest that you were being well fed and treated kindly, as we were passing.' She smiled at one and then the other trying to lighten the mood.

Her father's brow creased. 'Passing here? Where, pray, were you passing to and from? What are you doing travelling around the country, unchaperoned it appears, with this . . . stranger?' He leaned forward to her.

'I have taken employment in his service. He is a surgeon and I am going to help him establish a hospital, Father.' Felicity tried to sound confident, but as her father rose to his feet and stood before Lucas, she was starting to believe that this visit may not have been at all wise.

'Why are you not still under the care of my good friend, Julian Cannon?' he asked.

'I had to find alternative accommodation. His attentions changed from employer to . . . ' she hesitated and saw her father's colour flush, 'He tried to be too friendly, Father. Miss Richards wrote to Mr Packman recommending me for a position as his assistant.'

Squire Moon placed a hand on her shoulder. 'He did what? Employer, what nonsense is this?' His attention moved from Lucas to her. 'Felicity, did he . . . ? Has he . . . ?' His face was turning puce as he stumbled for the words he wanted to ask.

'The man made an ungentlemanly suggestion to her and Miss Richards, his housekeeper, thought it wise to seek an alternative position for Miss Moon's own safety,' Lucas replied. 'So now that you know your father is well, I shall give you some moments alone, and then we really must be going. I have no wish to cross the moors in the dark or spend another night at an inn.' Lucas stood up but was prevented from leaving as Squire Moon's hand gripped his arm.

'What do you mean — another night?' Her father looked from one to the other. It was obvious that they had taken a mutual dislike to each other.

'I mean, sir, that we must soon be on our way, if your daughter is to arrive safely in my home. I shall give her my protection until you are at liberty again and in return she will be of use within my establishment.' He placed his hand over her father's and pulled it away.

'You abuse her in any way and I shall be your undoing!' Her father snapped out the words bitterly, in a voice that Felicity hardly recognised. She thought how much he must have changed with the cruelty of the slur upon his name.

'Father, Mr Packman may be able to help you in your quest to clear your name. He is a gentleman.' Felicity saw the ironic look in her father's eyes, which appeared to be greeted by equal scepticism in those of Lucas. He picked up his bag and stepped towards the unlocked doors.

'Ten minutes, Miss Moon, then we must leave.' He stepped outside and Felicity turned to her father and smiled up at him.

He took both her hands in his. 'Tell me, Felicity, did you flirt with Julian at all? He is a man of the world, and you do not understand it yet.'

Felicity's cheeks flushed with hurt pride that he would ask such a question of her. 'No, he was worse for drink and I think he thought he would take advantage of one of his maids as he was inclined to do. I don't know for sure if at the time he even recognised who I was until I struck him.'

'You are not one of his maids! You were never supposed to be.' His voice rose. Then he patted her shoulder. 'You did right to strike the blackguard.'

'No, sir, I was not a maid. I helped the housekeeper.' Felicity was surprised to see his temper becoming worse.

'The bloody rogue! I'll sort out Julian Cannon, you see if I don't. I paid him good money to take you in until I sorted this mess out. I had no intention of you becoming a skivvy! Tell me about this shady character who has brought you here. Did you stay a night at an inn with him?' His grip was tightening.

'Father, you can do nothing to anyone whilst you are in here. The coach was involved in an accident and Mr Packman and I were nearly caught out in a storm so we did take shelter at an inn. It was out of necessity not by desire, and he is an absolute gentleman.' Felicity pulled her hands free.

'Your reputation lies in ruins, girl;

such stupidity, such naivety and treachery. I will bring Cannon to book for this.' He shook his head in desperation. 'What a mess!'

'Father, do not upset yourself. I shall be working, willingly, at Marram Hall with Mr Packman. We can communicate from there. It will work out for the best and once your appeal has been heard you shall be free to see the work we have done.'

'Marram Hall!' He tilted his head back and then stared at her, running his fingers through his thinning hair. 'Felicity, you do not know that man or what he is capable of. Trust me, do not take all you see and hear from him at face value. Yes, he is clever and you are naïve. Listen to my words. Take care, be on your guard and lock your door each night. Marram Hall is not a place I would have you within twenty miles of. I will be out of here one day. Hopefully, within months if all goes well, and then, girl, you will return home with me. We shall restore both our names and you will be found a husband. Don't trust that man, Felicity!'

She stared into his eyes. There was a genuine panic within him.

'I shall take care, Father. Unless, I could stay here . . . if there is another room I could have.' She looked around the walls.

He sighed loudly. 'You have no idea in life. Felicity, this is a gaol, surrounded by a barracks. Go and play at being a nurse, stay safe and I shall send out word as you go. You will be watched.'

'Send word to whom? Who will watch me?' She stared at him as he sat back down and picked up his quill, dipping it into the ink.

Lucas opened the door. 'Miss Moon, we need to leave now.'

She looked at his tall figure as he filled the doorway; so straight of back, but could she trust him? Her father said not.

She leaned over and kissed her

father's forehead. 'Take care, and write to me, please.'

He patted her hand. 'I will, now go. There is no time for sentiment in this world, girl.'

She was aware of him watching her leave. Lucas entered the room to retrieve his bag.

'I don't know what your game is, Packman, but you don't fool me with your high and mighty ways. You touch her and I'll have your hands surgically removed.' Moon's words were whispered to Lucas.

'Good day, Mr Moon. It will be a pleasure to care for your daughter; do not worry yourself, sir.' Lucas bowed to him, and as his head lowered towards Moon's he whispered, 'Do not waste your threats on me, sir.'

Felicity watched Lucas turn and smile at her as he met her at the doorway of the room. 'Come, Miss Moon, we have much work to do.' He escorted her out and closed the door turning the key within the lock as he did. They were greeted by the sergeant in his office.

'Everything, fine, I hope?' the man asked.

'Splendid, sir,' Lucas replied. 'Thank you for your time.'

The sergeant escorted them to the gig.

They pulled away; Felicity could see her father's figure watching the court-yard as they left.

'Are you satisfied now, Miss Moon?' Lucas asked.

'Yes, thank you,' she lied. Her mind now had more worries than before. Why should she not trust the man she sat next to? He had proved himself to be a gentleman. When would her father be free? Why did she have to be married off? How had he managed such comfort in gaol? It was all deeply unnerving, yet she was starting a new phase in life. It would be exciting, if only it could be trusted as genuine, like the man beside her.

6

Lucas drove the gig as if he were in a desperate rush to reach Marram Hall. There was no time or opportunity for conversation as she held fast to the seat. He handled the vehicle with skill as they crossed the vale; it climbed the steep rise to the open moor road and then branched off on to what appeared to be a lonely track headed towards the sea.

On the far horizon, billowing smoke of large fires reached up into the sky. 'What is that?' she asked, as the gig finally slowed, the horse being allowed to walk at a steady pace after its exertions.

'Don't worry about that. It is the alum mines they're burning off to collect the liquor. It's long, arduous process, but essential to retrieve the mineral. However, we do not travel so far. We go down here.' He gestured to a turning off their track.

They branched onto a narrow road that led steeply down to a sweeping sandy bay. Felicity held on to her hat as the north-easterly wind blew in over the German sea. The land ahead descended at an increasingly severe angle causing Felicity to hang on to the seat again with her other hand.

When Lucas brought the gig to a halt Felicity was greatly relieved. She looked up at him wondering why he should bring her to such a wild place. The steep overgrown cliffs fell away to a distant sandy beach on which cobles were lined up with the fishermen busy alongside sorting their catch and the women and children tending the nets and lobster pots. She could just see the roofs of a scattering of huts on the edge of the flat sandy beach. Opposite, nestled against the ragged cliffs, was a ramshackle collection of houses. Their red-pantiled roofs seemed in stark contrast to the greenery behind them, or the sandy rocky outcrops.

He stared down at her. 'Look to your left.' Felicity turned her head and saw that standing out along the land framing the north of the bay was a row of trees behind which a track opened up leading to a grey castellated building upon the headland. It stood stark and strong, reminding her of the asylum and gaol in Gorebeck. She remembered her father's warning not to trust this man.

'That is Marram Hall. It belonged to a man who used to own one of the alum mines. He was bent on wealth and abused his power. He was caught and brought to justice. Now he is in gaol.' He was still staring at her as if he was making some point of reference to her father.

'My father is innocent. You see the way they treat him. They must know it or else he would have been thrown into the cells.' She looked at him defiantly.

'He has luxury because he can afford to buy it and the sergeant accepts bribes. Poor men, innocent or not, will groan alone in the cells.' He looked at the reins in his hand.

'Is that what you would wish for my father, too?' The sharpness of her retort caused her to look up quickly.

'I would not wish it on any innocent person, Miss Moon.' He manoeuvred the horse onto the track and they made their way across the headland in the relative shelter of the trees. The view of the crashing waves across the bay was the most dramatic scenery Felicity had ever seen. She breathed in the salt-laden air and felt it refresh her lungs. This was so different to the calm of the country air that she was used to.

They stopped in front of the building. Felicity did not know what it was she had come to; a derelict building, an existing hospital or an empty shell filled with its ghosts and memories of previous owners. This was so far removed from the Jacobean manor house she had grown up in that she felt as though she was about to enter a whole new world.

'Welcome to my home, Miss Moon. I hope you shall find it comfortable.' He looked at her and smiled genuinely for what was the first time since they had met. 'This place grows on you. The air is clean and the water supply plentiful. Come and I shall show you my dream.' He jumped down from the gig without using the footplate, as a boy ran out of the house and took the horse's reins.

'James, this is Miss Moon. She will be my new assistant. Tell Cook I have returned and we require a hot meal for two. But first we shall have tea in the day room as soon as possible.' He patted the lad's back before helping her down. The boy smiled broadly at him, in an easy manner.

He took hold of her hand and led her up the few stone steps to the main door. This he opened wide revealing, to Felicity's great surprise, an interior filled with natural light. She stepped inside onto a marble tiled floor and stared above her at the large window high in the roof. The building, although square in design, had a central quadrangle that was framed by broad sweeping stairs, but the entrance hall itself was shielded by a central glass dome high above them. This was protected on the outside by the castellated roof, it let a shaft of light straight through the core of the building. The effect was stunning.

When she turned around and faced Lucas she saw him standing leaning against the wall watching her.

'It is marvellous, Mr Packman. Totally unexpected!'

'Yes, it is. It is irony at its best. Cold and sinister on the outside, yet behind these doors light and refreshing. Come into the day room. We shall have a warm drink then I shall show you the rooms. Your own will be on the second landing. The first will be reserved for patients and the lower rooms for servants. You shall have no need to venture beyond the ground floor. Store rooms are of no interest to a young lady.' He opened the oak door to a room that was a hotchpotch of morning room and library. Again, the natural light illuminated the room as it filtered through three tall rectangular windows, each made of a number of smaller panels. The view out over the bay and sea was breathtaking. She walked straight over to the central window, lost in thought. It was like looking at ever changing scenery. Then, as she looked at the edge of the window she realised that there were two windows mounted in a broad frame within the wall.

'Quite clever,' she spoke her thoughts aloud.

'I'm glad you think so.' He came and stood next to her. 'One layer would have been very draughty so I had them make two frames. It was a luxury I allowed myself in order to enjoy such a magnificent view.'

Looking around the room which was richly hung with drapes, tapestries and had a Turkish carpet in front of a warm open fire, she thought he did not exactly go without his creature comforts.

A short lady bustled into the room with the tea tray.

'Sir, if you'd sent word I'd have had a meal ready for thee already.' The woman stopped and looked at Felicity. 'Be this the Moon girl?' she asked sharply.

'Mrs Shepherd, kindly refrain from using that tone of voice. This is Miss Moon, who will be my new assistant. You will show her some respect!' He was talking to her sternly yet at the same time appeared to be tolerating the woman's rude behaviour.

'If you say so, Mr Packman. I'll try for your sake,' she looked over to Felicity, 'I'll see to yer room later.' She turned and left them without pausing to see if Lucas required anything else.

'Why should she be so rude to me?' Felicity asked, annoyed at the cook's attitude.

'Ignore her.' Lucas looked out of the window.

'What, without understanding her ill manners?' Felicity was adamant that she would be treated with respect.

He looked at her, staring into her deep blue eyes. 'Is it so important? Can you not just concentrate on your work here?'

'It is important to me.' Felicity was indignant.

'Very well. Your father, Squire Moon, turned her man off his land when he became ill and could not pay his tenancy. He died and she is a bitter woman. I saved her from the same fate when I arrived here by taking her in and giving her work.'

Felicity could not believe what he had said. 'My father would not have done such a thing. There would have to be another reason.' She stared at him, desperately hoping he would listen to her and not the spiteful, lying tongue of such a wench.

'You asked the reason. I have given it to you. If you cannot accept it that is up to you. As far as I am concerned it is a closed matter and we have more important issues with which to occupy ourselves.' He sat in a chair by the fire. 'Come and have your tea then I will show you the hall.'

'You do not believe me? My father is . . . '

'Innocent, you have told me already, I believe. Felicity let me give you some advice. Whilst you are here you may discover more about your father than you are aware of so far. Nothing, though, must come between you and your work. I need to establish this place and shall be fetching patients here within two weeks. You shall focus on that and put all personal matters aside. I shall not have my staff at war with each other. Is that clear?' He poured her tea and offered it to her.

She took it graciously. 'Yes, quite.' Felicity sat down in the other chair. Sipping the tea quietly she listened to him relate the specifics of her duties and explain how soon he hoped to have the hospital open. He was undoubtedly handsome, and as Lucas warmed to his topic his eyes shone with enthusiasm and life, but one thought permeated her mind and that was the words of her father. Do not trust all he says. He had just lied to her, as if trying to set her against her own kin. She would be on her guard and await her father's release. Then he would see he really was innocent.

7

Felicity loved her room. It was nothing like the servants' bedroom she had shared with three other girls at Mister Cannon's home. Her window overlooked the sweep of the bay. Within days she realised that life for the fishermen and their families was one of continuous toil. They physically pulled the boats out to the relentless waves, even at night, over what were violent and treacherous seas. Felicity arose early, received a basic breakfast given in silence under the hateful eyes of Mrs Shepherd, and then spent the day working diligently in the shadow of Lucas as he showed her the rooms, medicines, sheets and essentials needed for the hospital. Men finished whitewashing the last of the store rooms and at last Lucas seemed happy that all was ready for the first private patients who were arriving within days. It was difficult for Felicity not to be affected by his enthusiasm.

There was one room she was frightened of and did not relish entering and that was the one where his surgical skills would be used. Partly because, until she had experienced this side of his treatment, she had no way of knowing how she would react to it. It was here that she had been sent to place a bucket of sand in the corner of the room.

She heard the door open behind her and turned, smiling, as she expected to see Lucas standing there. Felicity did not want him to sense her fear, for she was determined to fulfil her role as efficiently as Edna would have. However, she was surprised to see Mrs Shepherd standing in the doorway almost sneering at her.

'Girl, you don't belong 'ere. You don't want to get those dainty fingers dirty in a place like this. Just think of all the blood, guts and worse that'll be spilled as he slits into the wretches' flesh. There's ghosts 'ere too. Why don't you go get yerself a job as a governess or some such nice position and leave Mr Packman alone. He's not the marryin' sort. He's married to his work, he don't need the likes of you — a goaled man's brat.' The woman folded her arms and stared down her nose at Felicity. She was a big strong woman, but Felicity was not scared of her.

'How dare you talk to me so? You don't know me. You tell lies about my father and you are presumptuous in the extreme.' Felicity faced her. 'Do not judge everyone by your own standards and manners or should I say the lack of them.' Felicty could see by the woman's expression that she had surprised her. Mrs Shepherd had obviously decided she was a fragile creature who could be bullied and frightened with vengeful words.

'You mean yer not after him? Then why else are you 'ere? Don't tell me yer old man could not afford a decent home for you until he buys himself out of trouble.' The vitriol in the woman's words stung Felicity, but she tried hard not to show it.

'I mean, Mrs Shepherd, whether I like Mr Packman or not is none of your business. My feelings for Mr Packman are exactly that — mine, and none of your concern. So be about your business and take that long snout of yours out of mine!' Felicity was about to launch into a further tirade at the woman when Lucas appeared behind her.

'Ladies, when you have finished talking perhaps you could complete your given tasks. Mrs Shepherd, I believe the kitchens are downstairs. I require you to prepare luncheon.' He looked at her and she lowered her eyes.

'Sorry, sir, I just wanted to see how the room looked now as it's finished.' She meekly walked away.

'Felicity,' he lowered his voice and she grasped her hands in front of her to calm the embarrassment she felt. Had he heard her words? If so, what on earth would he be thinking of her? She had not meant to say anything in such a way that could be misconstrued as to her having intentions upon him. The ferocity within her own outbreak had taken her by surprise as well as Mrs Shepherd. She just wanted to put the woman in her place.

He continued, 'I do not enjoy conflict between my staff. It is my request to you that you find a way of making peace with Mrs Shepherd. She is a good woman who works hard. We would be sadly inconvenienced should she leave.' He looked thoughtfully at her. 'Please, try and do this for me. We all need to work together, Felicity.'

'She is always so rude to me.' Felicity looked up at him. He had a way of watching her as if there was something more he wished to say, but some invisible force seemed to stop him. Instead the air between them was filled with an awkward silence, until he changed the subject and started to talk about his work again.

'She has a brusque manner. In time it will soften as she sees the person you really are,' he looked around the room, Felicity knew the subject would change back to the hospital now. 'We are ready.' His smile was broad and when his eyes returned to hers they were full of life and hope again.

'You are really committed to this. I shall do my level best not to undo your good work, but I will not stand by and have her insult myself or my family.' Felicity was adamant that the woman would be made to realise this.

'Did she insult you?' His question was not as straightforward as it seemed.

'She presumes too much about me.' She saw a flicker of humour in those deep brown eyes and knew instantly he had heard every word she had spoken.

'It is a shame then that I arrived when I did, for perhaps you were about to contradict her presumptions . . . Confess your intentions are purely . . . honourable.'

'Perhaps,' she added. 'However, my intentions are always honourable. It is others who discredit them.'

He leaned forward to her and was about to add further comment when there was a shout from the main hall. 'Mister Packman, there is a coach and a wagon arriving.'

Lucas's face showed sheer joy. 'It begins, Felicity! We are a hospital.' He took hold of her shoulders and, in the aura of the moment, kissed her lightly on the lips. Her eyes closed as she felt his mouth against hers. What was, she thought at first to be a momentary whim seemed to linger. She was returning his kiss and responding to his touch. The moment it ended they stared into each other's eyes. He removed his hands from her shoulders and walked to the doorway.

Felicity took one step toward him but stopped as he, too, hesitated. He looked back at her at a loss for words. 'I . . . Pardon . . . ' His cheeks were slightly coloured.

'Your patients await, Mr Packman.' She smiled at him and he nodded to her before running down the stairs to the hallway taking two steps at a time.

Felicity took a deep breath, controlling the emotions that were confusing her body and mind and made her way calmly down the stairs to join him, aware that the real work was about to begin.

8

Felicity saw the huge wagon pull up outside the building. Two groundsmen came from the stables and helped to unload its burden. She watched as Lucas walked further along the drive waiting for the coach to arrive, leaving her, Mrs Shepherd and Ambrose to see to the goods. As bed frames were lifted down, Felicity smiled. These were no normal beds, they were small. Then a number of stacked cots were lifted onto the steps.

'Silas, you and James start carrying the cots up to the rooms. Mrs Shepherd, Felicity and Ambrose take the linen, food and medicines through to the store rooms. We shall organise them when all is safely inside.'

He glanced up towards the darkening sky, which ominously appeared as if rain was imminent and walked toward the slowing coach.

'They're beds for children. It is to be a children's hospital!' Felicity said enthusiastically, as she lifted up a bundle of pillows.

'Quick, isn't she?' Mrs Shepherd remarked to Ambrose, tilting her bonneted head in Felicity's direction.

Ambrose, a man Felicity had not seen before, half smiled at the woman. Felicity looked sternly at her. The man's impassive face remained unchanged. Felicity guessed he was from the local village. His skin looked as though he was used to being exposed to the elements, like a fisherman would be.

'Mrs Shepherd, you will treat me with the same courtesy that you would expect me to show you,' Felicity replied directly to her as they walked inside the hall.

'Good, then I don't have to change owt, do I?' the woman answered, 'because I don't expect you to be any different to me than your pa was. He sure treat us bad.' She did not give

Felicity the chance to reply, and led the way to the store rooms.

Felicity was aware of Lucas greeting people from the coach, and realised this was not the time or place to take the Shepherd woman down a peg or two. So, dutifully, she concentrated on the job in hand.

This was the first time that Felicity had entered the lower rooms. The stone store rooms were along a passage in the shape of a lower quadrangle below the main building. Lamps lit the corridor from which all the doors led off.

Mrs Shepherd walked to the fourth door. There were others further along but she turned around and blocked the way. 'These are the rooms we use; bedding and medicines are all in the first one. There is no need for you to go further than that.' Shepherd folded her arms.

'What are they used for?' Felicity asked, and pointed to the rooms further along.

'They aren't. Now we have work to

do. It may be a word you are unused to but I'm sure in time you'll learn to be of some use here.' The woman stared at her, leaning forward. 'I'm sure Mr Lucas shall think of something, eh?'

'Whilst we are here, Mrs Shepherd, I want you to know that my father is innocent of the crimes listed against him. Once he is free I shall speak to him about the circumstances of your husband's tenancy.' Felicity was trying to sound both calm and confident. 'Be careful of how far you go, Mrs Shepherd, Mr Packman is no fool, and he sees people clearly as they are.'

Shepherd took two steps toward her. 'You listen good to me, Miss. My Jack died because he was ill made homeless by your old man. Do yer know what I really wish, eh? Well, it's simple as this: I hope your father rots in that cell of his. He put us out in the middle of winter. No, lass, if the truth be told I hope he rots in hell.' She pushed past Felicity knocking her against the wall.

Felicity was shaken by the woman's

anger. There was no getting through to her. Deep inside she felt a twinge of something, possibly unease. The thought of her father, so warm and cosy in the room at the gaol was so far removed from what the woman presumed to be the case; as she herself had. There was no equitable contrast with his circumstance and that of being made homeless. Her heart felt heavy, yet she could not believe this picture that was being slowly painted of her father. He was a gentleman, not a felon.

A noise from the far end of the corridor caught her attention. she looked back and could just hear Lucas and strangers talking in the main hallway but no sign of Shepherd returning. She inched her way toward the door at the end of the passage.

Nervously, she passed each flickering lamp in turn. The door was on the corner of the corridor. She reached out her hand for the large iron handle but, as she did, the lamp nearest to her went out. Felicity found herself alone in pitch darkness. Each of the three lamps that had illuminated the corridor had been extinguished silently; leaving the nearest until last so that she would be deserted in the cold blackness of the unlit corridor. So intent had she been on the door, she had been totally unaware of anyone else's presence.

She turned around. 'Who's there?' she asked.

Behind her she thought she heard shuffling from within the room. Ahead of her she could just see something move in the shadows. A figure retreating. Fear started to take hold. She forced herself to walk slowly back towards the noises in the main hall.

As she came level with the first store room, Mrs Shepherd appeared in front of her, her arms filled with sheets.

'Whatever are yer playing at, girl?' the woman snapped at her as she stared into the darkness.

'Do you think I'm scared of the dark, Mrs Shepherd?' Felicity's anger was conquering the fear. 'Or you for that matter? Playing such foolish pranks is child's play, woman.'

'Hold these, whilst I sort out the lamps.' Mrs Shepherd literally dumped her load onto Felicity whilst she fetched her tinder box.

Once the lamps were lit again, she reclaimed the goods.

'I ain't got time to play games, Miss Moon. So looks like you've got someone else 'ere who doesn't want yer here either. Best take care, lass — or better still, leave.' She took the goods into the store room, shouting back, 'Mister Packman wants you. Best go where you're wanted whilst yer still can.'

Felicty felt like slamming the door shut on the woman and seeing how she felt alone in the dark, but that would be petty so she sought out Lucas. She was sure she had heard noises from the unused rooms, though. For now she let it be, but at some time in the future she would return to find out what it had been. Her father had warned her about this house and she was beginning to believe his words were true. It was a house of secrets, as was Mr Lucas Packman, but what?

In the main hall Lucas stood with a group of four women. They were dressed similarly in what looked to be a standard travelling coat, boots and carrying identical bags.

'Miss Moon, these ladies will be our nurses. They have had a reasonable education and basic training. We shall be receiving three long stay patients tomorrow. They will arrive separately and these ladies will have the bulk of their care. Could you see them to their rooms, please, and then attend me in my study whilst they have time to refresh from the journey. Mrs Shepherd will prepare a meal for them to eat in the kitchen.' He turned to the nervous looking young women. 'Ladies, if you follow Miss Moon, she will show you to your rooms.'

He returned to the store rooms with Ambrose.

'This way,' Felicity addressed them and led them upstairs.

By the time she returned to the library she knew their names and had found out they had been selected from a school by Lucas. He had taken them to a London hospital where they had served as nurses for three months before undertaking the journey north.

She knocked on the library door and waited until he told her to enter.

He was standing in his waistcoat and shirt sleeves, leaning against his desk.

'Mr Packman, they are very happy with the room, but very tired after the long journey.' She closed the door behind her.

'That's to be expected on both accounts. Felicity, I shall explain briefly about our initial clients here. They are three children — one baby and two young children, whose parents are ashamed of them and who are willing to pay for them to be hidden away from the world. The baby is a bastard child of a powerful man's daughter. He is, as far as I know, healthy and shall be here long term. The other two are in need of help. One has a limp, the other stammers uncontrollably. Both of these children can be helped. The money that I am accepting to house and treat these few will pay for a number of children to be helped from the poor. We shall only survive by a reputation of discretion and secrecy. I hope you will honour this. I do not wish for you to inadvertently mention whom these abandoned children are, should you discover the families concerned. I will officially be adopting them for a fee.' He stopped speaking and looked at her, waiting for her response.

'There is no one here I could tell,' she replied, not sure what he was expecting her to say.

'No, there isn't, but I do not wish your father to have this knowledge. This is to be seen simply as a hospital. I am asking you to respect my wishes and not to correspond on this matter with your father. Will you give me your word, Felicity?'

'You do not trust my father is a man of honour?' Felicity saw his brow rise, but he did not reply.

'I shall not break your trust, sir. But my father is in no position to act on any such information even if he felt so inclined, is he?' Felicity asked.

'Your father has a deal of liberty and means at his disposal. Let us not put temptation in his way. Agreed?' He looked at her and smiled.

'Agreed,' Felicity said, and he looked instantly relieved. 'I am pleased you at least trust me . . . sir.'

He laughed and his face filled with an impish grin. So different from the serious façade it showed to the world. He placed a hand on her shoulder and walked back to the door with her. 'Come, I shall show you the children's rooms and we shall eat in the day room together.'

She glanced up at him, unsure of his intentions.

'That way we can discuss how we are to go about finding the children who most need my help.'

He removed his hand and opened the door. Ambrose was standing in the hallway as they alighted. Lucas walked straight past him but the man turned and winked knowingly at Felicity in a manner that made her feel uneasy.

9

When Squire Moon opened his letter from his daughter he was in fine spirits. He was proud of Felicity and how she had made the most of their change in fortunes. He was pleased also that the man, Packman, appeared to be keeping his word and focussing on his work, and off Felicity. He sucked on his pipe and relaxed by the fire relieved, that within the next few months at least, she had found a safer place to live than the one he had misguidedly left her in. Once out he would make his first priority — no, his second; his first would be to take revenge — to find her a husband and rebuild her reputation. There was many a man of rank hit hard by bad luck, losing a fortune at the gambling clubs of London.

It would not be long now and his release would be secure, then he could take her home and they could put this whole unpleasant business behind them. He would, in time, make everything right once more. When he read on, his peace of mind was shattered. Moon's attitude changed.

Father there is someone here who concerns me. She is a cook by the name of Shepherd. Her husband was a tenant on your land and she claims that they were turned out of their cottage in mid-winter. Father, I don't know why she says such things. The man died and she is a bitter woman toward us, but for the sake of the children we work silently together whenever necessary. Please could you explain what happened or why this person is such a liar?

The letter continued with news of the progress they had made; of unwanted brats who were becoming little angels in the eyes of his gullible daughter. Her attachment sounded too much for him, not to mention the admiration and respect she had for Packman, her words glowing with pride and enthusiasm for the change they had made to their first patients. But all this was lost on Moon. He stood up and shouted loudly, 'Damnation! Is there no end to my torments?' He screwed up the letter into a ball and flung it into the back of the fire.

Moon realised he had no choice; he would have to take a great risk. He went over to the door and hammered on it loudly. 'Sergeant! Sergeant!' Was there no end to his nightmare? 'People will pay for this,' he swore bitterly.

The sergeant opened the door and entered as Squire Moon stomped up and down the room in clearly bad temper.

'I need to be free for two, maybe three days and I need to leave here tonight!' He stood in front of the sergeant who merely scratched his head, looking bemused at this sudden demand.

'I cannot allow that. You would risk everything you have tried to achieve. It is more than my rank is worth, sir, should an internee be caught at large.

How would I explain such an event unless I said you had escaped? Even then I would look a complete imbecile. No, sir, it cannot be achieved.' He turned to leave.

'I will pay you, man. Help me. My daughter is in danger and I need to help her.' Squire Moon tried to look as desperate as he felt.

The sergeant smiled. 'Perhaps I could send my men if you explain yourself,' the man persisted, but Moon could see the tell tale glint of interest in his bloodshot eyes.

'That would not do. This is a personal issue that I should have dealt with long since. By the gods, I thought I had, yet it comes back to haunt me once more.'

'Perhaps there is a way, but it will cost you dear, sir, and if it is discovered you are at liberty then you are on your own. You will be an outlaw or spend years in gaol for real. I mean cells, man — cold, damp and prison rations.'

'I appreciate the risk, but I must do

this.' Squire Moon was almost pleading with the man.

'There is a prisoner who suffers from the damp and cold. I am sure he would stay here, as you, and even pretend you have a chill and need more bed rest than normal, just for a couple of days in order to have the use of a good bed and a warm fire. He's about your build. He does not even need to know why he has been moved. Could be out of the kindness of my own heart; no need for him to speak to no one. I will have to be on duty for most of the time and that will cost. I'm risking my neck here, Squire.'

'You'll have your reward but I need a horse, my pistol and I go tonight.' He stared at the sergeant.

'I'll come for you as soon as darkness falls. But listen to me, Moon, you be back by daybreak in two days' time or I'll set the dragoons looking for you. Understand? And I'll still collect my pay.' He was waving a stubby finger in Moon's face.

'I give you my word and you swear that I've been here the whole time. For when I return I don't want any new accusations listed against me. A gaoled man cannot commit any crimes.'

The sergeant opened the door. 'Take care, sir. Your luck has held out to date, but never press providence too far.'

Squire Moon did not answer. He watched the man leave having had the last word. For he needed him now, but the day would soon come when he didn't and that moment could not come soon enough for Squire Moon.

★ ★ ★

'Hannah! Take off your clothes now and stop being such a silly girl. It's time you had a wash in the tub, lass. Now stop being such a fool and let's be 'aving yer.'

'I . . . I . . . I . . . don't . . . ' Hannah tried to speak but the words stopped in her throat.

Mrs Shepherd stood with arms

crossed and a chunk of soap in her hand. She had been told by Felicity to fetch the tub up for Hannah and she had no patience for her at all. 'Come on you buffoon, don't yer understand words, let alone know how to speak them? When I say do something, yer do it!'

The girl stood shaking in her nightdress not moving at all. Shepherd took one step towards her as the door opened and Felicity arrived.

'Thank you, Mrs Shepherd, for fetching the tub. I'll take over now. I believe Mr Packman needs you to attend young William.' Felicity smiled, but it was artificial and the woman threw the piece of soap into the tub as she passed by, making sure it caused the water to splash Felicity's apron. Felicity waited until the door was closed and then walked calmly over to Hannah. The girl, no more than ten, was like a frightened shadow.

'Hannah, it is safe here. I'll make sure Mrs Shepherd does not come near you again. She is brusque. Her manner is coarse, but she will not harm you. No one here will beat you. This is your home now.'

The girl did as she always did when Felicity reassured her, and simply hugged her. Felicity had managed to reach this child who needed no surgery, but just love and understanding. She had a slight limp and a stammer; her family disowned her as a freak, but Felicity saw only a lost, frightened child, who had a beautiful face and a gentle nature. Lucas had left her care in the hands of Felicity and already she was putting on some weight, and occasionally managing whole sentences without one stammer.

'Now, before that water goes cold, why don't you climb in whilst I sit over there and read to you.' The chair that Felicity had pointed to was by the door and away from the eye line of the tub so that the girl had her privacy. Hannah nodded so Felicity left a piece of towel by the tub and her clothes on the bed. She picked up the novel and started to read. That way Hannah knew her eyes were focussing on the words and this apparently made her feel safe because she also knew that she wasn't alone. Felicity loved this house. The work was so rewarding and Lucas was the kindest of men. He helped the poor children with as much diligence as he did those who were his paying 'guests'. Hannah was one of whom he was becoming the legal guardian.

The only person who spoiled Felicity's happiness was Mrs Shepherd. There was no removing the woman's hostility toward her. She hid it from Mr Packman but took every opportunity to display it openly when Felicity was alone. But the woman worked hard and Lucas relied on her.

Two chapters later, Hannah was dry, dressed and ready to go and play with William, a child who had had an operation on his leg and was learning to walk on it again. The two children had formed a strong bond between them.

As Hannah entered the room, Lucas was just leaving.

'Felicity, I need some fresh air. Would you care to take a walk with me?' He looked a little unsure of himself as he asked her.

'Yes, of course,' Felicity answered and unwrapped her apron.

'Good, downstairs in ten minutes.' Lucas walked off and Felicity went and fetched her coat. She ran down the stairs to the main hall and saw Ambrose entering the corridor to the store rooms. The opportunity to explore the mysterious sounds from the end room had not presented itself. She stopped, looking in the direction that he had gone.

'Ready?' Lucas's voice surprised her and she jumped slightly when he spoke.

He smiled broadly at her.

'Yes, sorry, I was just waiting.' He opened the outside door and they stepped out of the hall together into the bracing air.

* * *

The door was closed firmly behind them by Mrs Shepherd, who immediately followed after Ambrose, grateful that Mr Packman had got the Moon woman out of their way.

10

Lucas placed his arm around Felicity's shoulders as he steered her away from the prevailing wind and into the shelter of the avenue of trees that lined the headland.

'There, once you turn your back to the 'sea breeze' you can actually hear yourself speak.' His hair was blown forward over the high collar of his long coat, the locks framing his face. He was almost laughing.

She had tied her bonnet on tightly and looked up at him to see his eyes staring down at her.

'You are really happy here, aren't you, Mr Packman?' He was walking her towards a point between the trees that overlooked the bay beneath. Fishing boats bobbed up and down on the waves below as they brought their catch ashore. The women and children all gathered on the beach to help land the fish.

At first she thought that he had not heard her, for he leaned against a tree and stared out over the sweeping stretch of sand.

'Yes, I do. There is fresh air here away from the squalor and stench of the city.'

She looked to the far skies where the alum fires still burned, and then to the horizon that was littered with collier ships going up and down the coast from between the mines of the north, from Tyne to the Thames. 'It is a very busy place, the sea, yet here we are remote,' she mused, as she stood just behind him sheltered from the wind. 'Did you work in the city?' she asked.

He looked at her as if deciding what he should tell her or how much. 'I lived in the city. I worked for a time on the hulks, Felicity.'

She looked at him waiting for him to explain what he meant. When he did not enlarge upon the subject she had to ask further, 'What are 'Hulks'?'

His shoulders slumped as he put his hands deep into the pockets of his coat. 'You have a naivety and vulnerability about you that I would hate you to lose. Your reputation, which has no doubt suffered grievously by your father's misdeeds and by your association with me, has been most unfairly damaged.'

'My father is innocent!' she said firmly.

He did as he always did when the issue raised its head and ignored any further reference to it. 'The hulks are literally the hulks of old Men-of-War that are moored at Portsmouth, Plymouth and on the Thames. They are filled with men, women and children convicted of many and various crimes; the most heinous and the innocent left cheek by jowl in a living hell. I was, for a brief period, employed to examine them as they arrived upon the vessels.' He stared out to sea. 'What I saw there I shall not describe to you. Suffice to say that it was what steered me towards buying Marram Hall.'

'Do they stay on them long?' Felicity asked, eager to keep him talking because she knew so little about him and desperately wanted to discover the truth. Perhaps her father had misunderstood his intentions. If she discovered more about the man she would inform her father in her next letter and try to gain some respect and understanding between the two of them. For she found she admired both and would have them befriend each other, if possible.

'Until they are transported to the colonies or New South Wales or they die in their own stench.' His mouth was set in a solemn line.

'It is a long way from the Thames to Marram Hall. Do you have family up here?' she asked him, but saw as he looked at her he felt he had already said too much. He did not appear to like exposing his emotions openly.

'We must return to our chores, Felicity. I will be going into the village this afternoon with Ambrose to see how one of the children is recovering. Will you try and bring Hannah out into the shelter of the trees? She needs to have fresh air to build up her strength. Take care she is well wrapped up.' He turned away from the sea to face her.

'Yes, of course, but . . . ' She hesitated, not wanting to bring up the subject of Mrs Shepherd again.

'But what, Felicity?' He gently stroked her cheek with his finger as she searched for the right words. She tilted her head to the warmth of his hand as he nestled her face in it. Since the moment a few weeks ago, when strange emotions had swept across both of them they had been totally respectful and professional in each other's presence.

'But,' she forced herself to think about Hannah, 'The girl is terrified of Mrs Shepherd.'

She tilted her head up to see if she had annoyed him by raising the topic of the woman's obnoxious manner again. His face was so close to hers that their lips met each other and once more all was lost of the world beyond them, other than the feel of warmth as he held her in his arms. It was not only warmth of his body shielding her from the elements but an inner glow that swept through her whole being. He pulled his head away, but still held her to him. She placed her cheek upon his coat, feeling the cold air on her face. He just seemed to be resting his head against her bonnet.

'Oh, Felicity, you are one complication I did not plan for, forgive me?' He released her from his embrace and she stepped back, her cheeks slightly flushed and her body shivering involuntarily as the cold air came between them.

'Complication, Lucas?' she repeated his words, questioning what he had said.

'I shall make sure that Mrs Shepherd does not go into Hannah's room if the girl is so sensitive to her practical manner.' He immediately turned to walk back to the hall. 'I must be on my way or I shall not be back for dinner.'

It was obvious that whatever had passed between them once more, Lucas was dealing with it the only way he knew how, by walking away from it. Felicity was not. She felt his need. He wanted her and she him. How long would he keep turning away from her? 'Mr Packman, tell me something, please, before you run off?' She had taken him by surprise. Her voice was firm, confident and it stopped him mid step. He faced her, obviously expecting her to question him over his actions. Once she had his full attention she took a step toward him.

He shrugged his shoulders at a loss for words.

'Tell me, what is in the other store rooms?' She saw the fleeting look of relief disappear as she had not pressed him for an explanation of his actions; instead a puzzled look crossed his face.

'The other store rooms are empty. They are damp and therefore of no use. That is why they are kept locked up.

Why do you ask?'

'Because of the noises,' she began to explain, but as Ambrose approached with the wagon, Lucas did not reply. He climbed up next to Ambrose.

'See to Hannah, Felicity,' he gave his instruction and immediately turned his attention to Ambrose, 'I thought you would have brought the gig.'

Felicity made her way to the hall; it was only as she climbed the steps that she looked back and saw that Lucas was still watching her.

11

Felicity was not ready to return to the hall. She ambled slowly in the general direction until the wagon was manoeuvred onto the bay road. Then she returned to the shelter of the trees where she could watch its descent. Ambrose was careful to steer the cumbersome vehicle down the steep road to the village.

She closed her eyes momentarily remembering the feel of Lucas's embrace around her body and the sensual warmth that had made her feel so secure in his arms. How could he be so personal towards her one moment and then so distant with her the next? He was, she decided, unclear in his thoughts about what he should do next. If he became involved with her, his life would become more complicated. So would hers, for that matter. Besides, she would have to consider her own feelings regarding his attention. Felicity smiled to herself. Perhaps he did not dare to speak of his feelings towards her in case she should turn him down. Many people find rejection hard, and he was such a private person. It was as though he was drawn to her, but he could not let himself acknowledge that he had fallen in love with her. Felicity decided it was time she helped him to make his mind up as to what his intentions were. If he should make another advance, she would resist her own temptation and insist he talk to her. They could not simply carry on as if nothing had happened between them other than a moment of madness. Whatever her father would think of his behaviour she had no idea. Since he had been imprisoned she had become exposed to the world in a way ill befitting the daughter of a squire. She opened her eyes again and breathed in deeply. It was an experience she had enjoyed because Felicity had learned to know her own mind; to experience the good and bad and to actually do things for herself. Helping at the hospital, particularly with Hannah, she had come to value her own efforts, her own ability to be of use to someone in need of her love and care, and in the process she had grown fonder of Lucas daily; this, despite her father's words of warning.

She saw the wagon reach the cottages at the edge of the sandy bay. A woman came out to greet Lucas; her gestures seemed erratic, that of a worried mother, Felicity guessed. He stepped down, collected his bag and was soon entering the cottage. She hoped the child would recover; it was heartbreaking to her to see children suffer.

Felicity glanced out to sea and saw that another boat had just been brought onto the water line. It caught her attention because all the others had been out and come back earlier. Felicity was about to turn around and return to the hall, when she saw Ambrose, who had been standing at the side of the wagon, lift a cover from the back of it. He slung a coil of rope around his neck and over one shoulder, then carried it down to the water's edge. There a man lifted it off him and placed it into the bottom of the boat. Felicity was intrigued. Next, a figure ran down to join them and almost launched himself into the coble next to the rope. Felicity did not see where the figure had come from, but suspected it was the youth, James, who helped up at the hall. He must have been in the wagon, she decided. But why did he not sit up and travel in comfort? Another heavy coil was placed in the coble and then the boat was pushed off. A fisherman took the oars and, as they put out to sea, Felicity could just make out the figure of James uncurl and sit up in the boat. Ambrose took out his clay pipe and returned to the wagon, walking it round the back of the cottages toward the stabling of the inn.

Felicity wondered what all the fuss was about. James had acted very strangely and for what? A couple of coils of old rope?' Tempted as she was to wait and watch for Lucas to leave the cottage, Felicity knew she would be missed and returned to the hall. She was glad to slip inside unnoticed by Mrs Shepherd who appeared to be busy shouting orders to the maid in the kitchens. She quickly returned to Hannah.

'Ah there you are, Hannah.' Felicity embraced the girl on entering the day room where she had been looking out of the window. Felicity wondered if she too had seen the boy in the boat. 'We're going for a walk, Hannah.'

The girl smiled at her, her mouth opened slightly as if she was going to speak, but then blushed slightly as she often did when she changed her mind. Felicity quickly wrapped her in a warm coat and a shawl, for she was slight of frame and susceptible to the chill. With a bonnet tied firmly upon her fair locks, Felicity led her back outside towards the shelter of the trees. Felicity slowed her pace to accommodate Hannah's uneven gait. She looked over to the cottages and smiled at the girl. 'Isn't it a lovely view?'

'N . . . n . . . not always,' the girl replied, staring anxiously down at the village.

'Why not always, Hannah? Why ever did you say that?' Felicity asked.

'P . . . p . . . pirates,' she said quietly, and held Felicity's hand tightly. 'In the . . . the night. I . . . I . . . hear them.' Hannah looked at the hall.

Felicity did not question her further because the girl looked so scared, but instead walked her along the path still holding her hand.

When Felicity glanced down to the road she saw Ambrose bringing Lucas and the wagon back up the steep bank. It amazed her how hard horses worked. The alum industry depended on horse and pony to cart the loads up and down the long slopes to the rutted rocky bays beneath where the boats waited. It was a hard life for both man and beast.

* * *

Squire Moon left the gaol dressed in the warden's overcoat and hat. He had to stoop quite low lest his tall figure attract unwanted attention. Once behind the building, hidden by the laundry shacks, he found his horse, pistol and coat. Quickly shedding his disguise, he led the horse out of the grounds by the river's tow path that passed behind the shacks and eventually joined the road through town just before the bridge. From there he wasted no time as he mounted and went at the gallop up onto the open moor road. He knew these roads as he did the ancient trods, like the lines upon his own hands.

Throughout his cold ride he fought with two different courses of action trying to make his choice. Time was short. He could sort out the Shepherds once and for all or he could pay a visit to his lecherous friend, Cannon, and scare the man senseless for daring to abuse his daughter so. As much as the latter course of action appealed to him it was the Shepherds who posed the greatest threat, so he headed for the coast.

On this moonlit night he made good speed. Marram Hall was on a headland exposed to the elements and difficult to approach unnoticed by land, but not by sea. He headed off the moor road to the tiny hamlet of fishermen's huts that were dotted on the edge of the marshes north of Stangcliffe. He needed help and he knew just the man — a man who owed him, and now it was time for him to collect on the debt.

★　★　★

The wagon rounded the steep turn at the top of the bay. Felicity had hold of Hannah's hand and, as the two men approached, she felt the child's grip tighten.

William looked very serious. Felicity realised straight away that his visit had not been successful. Ambrose chewed on his pipe as he drove the horse onwards. His face rarely changed. It seemed, to Felicity at least, that the weather had fixed the man's expression in a hard and unyielding manner. Whatever business he had had with James, it appeared that Lucas did not know anything about it.

'How was the child, Mr Packman?' she asked optimistically.

'As well as can be expected under the circumstances. Unfortunately, those circumstances are not good and the foolish ignorant parents refuse to let the child come up to the hall. They rant about ghosts and hobgoblins. So I am left to either treat the child in its hovel or abandon it. If it were the parents I should be tempted to but I can hardly blame the child for the father's shortcomings. God willing it may yet pull through.'

'I'll have Mrs Shepherd make up some broth and take it down later, eh, sir?' Ambrose suggested.

'Yes, but make sure it is the child who eats it, not the parents. Stay with them and watch if you need to.' He looked at Felicity and then to the hall. 'Do you wish to climb up on the back of the wagon?'

Hannah looked at her nervously after glancing at the back of Ambrose who had moved the wagon slowly forwards. The girl gripped her hand tightly.

'No, it is better that we have our exercise. I'll see you back at the hall, sir.' Felicity smiled at him and he nodded to her in return, conscious it would appear that they were not alone.

'Very well, come to my office when you return. There are matters I wish to discuss with you.' He looked at her, and this time it was she who nodded.

12

Squire Moon approached the hut on foot. He had tied the horse securely to a piece of driftwood washed up onto the sandy dunes that created a natural barrier between the sea and the marsh. With pistol drawn and bent double he crept through the small group of wooden huts until he was at the side of the one he sought.

Very slowly he placed his hand on the door's round handle. Glancing up he saw the tell tale smoke drifting out of the small chimney. That told him that the man he wanted was at home, but who else was with him he had no notion so he would have to just pray that they were not armed. Preferably the man would be drinking alone; if that was the case he was sure it would not be beyond his powers to overcome him if he tried to run. With pistol at the ready, he turned the handle until he heard the latch release inside, swiftly flinging the door wide open. He leaned against one side of the doorway as he pointed his pistol at the figure huddled on a rickety chair in the far corner.

The man's reactions were slow as he dropped the bottle of rum he had been drinking and fumbled for his gun.

Squire Moon's eyes scanned the cluttered hut; there was nothing but old rope, crab pots and a few half ankers of brandy against the far wall. Breathing easier with the knowledge that the man was alone, he stepped inside with confidence shutting the door behind him.

'Now then, Bernie, you're going to help me. I need an oarsman and you're one of the best in the business . . . so I've heard.'

Bernie looked as though he was going to try and run through the wall of the hut. Fear caused his slight frame to shake from head to foot. 'Squire, you heard wrong. Me nerve's shot. Was the war. You know I was pressed. Cannon fodder I was, on a man of war. Ain't no good no more.' He held out his shaking hand. 'Look, see!' The man stared at Squire Moon, with what was obviously supposed to be a look of honesty and innocence, qualities that had long since lost their powers on him.

'You're a bloody liar, Bernie. But that will not prevent you from rowing. Get up!'

Bernie looked calmly at the squire through half closed eyes. 'How the hell did you get here? I thought you was at the mercy of the turnkeys over Gorebeck way.' Bernie leaned against the wall and slumped into a defeated sitting position on the floor. Hugging his legs to his body he was trying to control himself and see through the blur of alcohol.

'I thought you'd be surprised to see me again. But you are going to help me. Not only to take me where I know you can, but to explain a few things to me en-route.'

'I don't know nothin'! I can't say nothin'! You're wastin' yer time comin' here. You should do a runner whilst you've still got the time to get away. How the hell did yer break out of that gaol? Or is it you want me to row yer down coast, eh? Whitby, Hull, even the Thames, eh?' His eyes widened as he looked around at the stashes of contraband in the hut. 'Damn it, man, are you sure you haven't brought the whole of the bleeding militia down here?'

Squire Moon grinned at the predictability of the man. His own skin first — well, he was going to have to risk it now, whether he liked it or not.

★ ★ ★

Once Felicity had taken Hannah back to her room, she had tried to warm the girl up with hot chocolate, hoping that as they sat and drank together she would relax and explain what she meant about the pirates. Felicity was

132

sure it would provide the key to her unsolved mystery of the noises from the store rooms. Each time Felicity had tried to go down that corridor, either Mrs Shepherd, Ambrose or James appeared, and she was forced to go into the first room to retrieve an item she really did not need. It was as though they controlled the ground floor. Hannah refused to speak of it again. As soon as Felicity mentioned 'pirates' Hannah shrank into herself and stared at the cup in her hand. So, Felicity decided, it was no good causing the child more distress. Instead, she left her to play with William in his room and went away with the reward of seeing the children's faces light up as they smiled at each other.

Felicity returned downstairs, and glanced at the entrance to the store rooms only to see Ambrose leaning idly against the entrance. He nodded at her but she made her way in the opposite direction and knocked on the door to Lucas's office.

She wondered what he wanted to speak to her about. Was he about to confide to her his feelings for her, personally opening his intentions to her, or was this summons to be about one more discussion regarding the provision of sheets, medicines and the importance of the patients' diets. Only time would tell.

* * *

'Bernie, get up. I need you and your boat. You're going to take me to Marram Hall . . . by sea.' The squire watched the man's face pale. His bottom lip quivered as he fought to speak and loosely pointed to the discarded bottle.

'I can't . . . I can't just, it's rough tonight . . . the rocks, they're killers. Besides, those steps haven't been used in the last twenty years. Hell, they may not even be there no more.' The man made no effort to stand.

Moon grabbed him by the collar and

dragged him to his feet, the pistol's barrel pressed against his jaw. 'Listen, you are no more important to me than the vermin that inhabit the filth of the earth. My daughter's in danger and you, man, are going to help me to remove that threat. If you do well, I'll reward you with a better life. If you don't, I give you my word as a gentleman, you won't have one to worry about. Do you understand me?' He shook the man as if he were no weight at all.

Bernie nodded so violently the tattered woollen hat that covered his greasy, lice ridden hair almost fell off. The squire released him letting him walk in front towards the beach.

'Wait!' he ordered, and the man stopped stock still. 'Release the horse's tether and walk him into the hut.' The pistol was trained on him.

'There's no room. He'll destroy everythin'.'

'The horse needs shelter. It's no weather to leave an animal out on the dunes.' He made the man manoeuvre the animal until it stood in the hut, as if it was in a stall.

Then he grabbed Bernie's coat at the shoulder and pushed him onwards over the soft-sanded dune and down to the firmer, wetter sand where his boat was chained up.

The cutting wind blew straight at the men's faces and it took both of them to push the boat physically out over the breakers and into the open sea. They climbed in and Bernie grabbed for the pistol that Moon had pushed into the drier safety of the boat whilst they put out to see. Despite the squire's maturity he was strong and quick. As the younger man focussed on the pistol, Moon grabbed the back of his coat and ducked his head over the side into the motion of the mass of water surrounding them. With one strong action he flung the man back into the boat, picked up the pistol and said one word, 'Row!'

13

Felicity entered Lucas's office. He was standing at the window opposite the door, looking out. She entered somewhat cautiously. He did not acknowledge her immediately but spoke quite softly. 'Close the door, Felicity, and please sit with me a while on the window seat.'

Felicity thought she saw a movement from the corridor across the entrance hall as she secured the door. Once seated, he flicked the tails of his coat out of the way and sat next to her. He was looking towards the door as he spoke, as if watching, keeping his voice low. 'Out there whilst we walked, Felicity, two things happened that intrigued me. I wish to speak to you about both of them.'

'Two things, sir?' she asked quietly.

'Yes, two and you can forget the 'sir'

when we speak alone together. We have crossed that line, 'Miss Moon', and we need to establish a very new and different one.' He looked into her eyes, his earnest expression touched her.

'What do you suggest?' she asked, and tried not to sound anything but serious, for she had no wish to make light of his conversation. It was just that, perched on the window seat together and almost whispering to each other in a conspirational fashion, she felt the urge to giggle, but that would be childish. Felicity realised she was feeling a strange mixture of nervousness and excitement. The situation was a new one to her.

'I suggest we deal with the second issue first. You said you heard noises from my empty store rooms. When did you? Which rooms do you allude to and what kind of noises?' he asked, and placed her hand in his. 'Don't be scared to speak out for I only wish to hear the truth.'

'I heard the noise of something being

dragged across the stone-flagged floor. I thought I may have heard a voice, but I'm not sure. I walked along towards the door to see what it was when the lamps were put out and I was left alone in the dark. I did not know what to do so I made my way quickly to the main store. I was scared because I didn't know who had extinguished the lamps and if there was anyone still there.'

She glanced out of the window to the sea beyond the headland. For a moment she thought she saw a little boat bobbing around on the waves, but then it disappeared from sight.

'Why did you not tell me of this earlier if it was something that disturbed you?' Lucas looked quite concerned. 'Anything untoward in this house should be immediately brought to my attention.'

'It is your house . . . your home. Whatever happens in here, I presumed you . . . ' she hesitated, looking down at their hands.

'You presumed I knew all about it or was even a party to it . . . whatever the 'it' is.' He nodded his head as if finding it a plausible and natural assumption. 'That would be a logical presumption to make. So, what would you believe of me if I told you that I thought those rooms to be empty, damp and unusable, what then? Would you believe me?' He made her look at him, face to face, by tilting her chin upwards gently in his hands.

'Yes, I would. But I don't believe in ghosts, Lucas. Neither do I believe my ears deceive me. My father said this place was dangerous and . . . ' She glanced back out of the window. There it was again, but no, perhaps not, sometimes the light played tricks on the eyes as the movement of waves forming made the sea rise and fall irregularly. If the boat existed at all it had vanished once more from her sight.

'And no doubt he warned you against its owner.' Lucas shook his head and she felt a stab of guilt because she had doubted him so much during the previous weeks.

'He was frightened for my safety, Lucas. Surely you understand why?' She defended her father's words. 'After all it is a highly irregular situation that we presented him with.'

'Tell me, Felicity, honestly, how did your father know so much about my home? How does he know you are in danger? How so?'

She withdrew her hand from his. 'He is a squire; an innocent man, who is worldly. He was in HM Navy. He is a man who has his eyes open to the ways of the world but has strong morals. He would never have deliberately jeopardised our home or my safety. If there is something about this hall that carries a bad reputation then he will be aware of it, but not a party to it. You want me to believe you — then I ask you this; can you believe me and my father? Trust has to be mutual or it is worthless, Lucas.'

* ★ ★ ★

The sea tossed the boat up and down the ever growing swells. The headland was a treacherous place but with skill the boat was rowed into the shelter of a cave on the bay side. It took the both of them to hold the coble steady until they could lash the rope to the iron pole that had been driven hard into the rock. Once they had done this they jumped with the motion of the water onto the rocky ledge at the bottom of a fixed ladder. This place was to Squire Moon the substance to many a tale he had heard in the local inns. He had fished these seas as a boy until one day his fortune and destiny changed his life forever. He had been pressed into service and ripped from his home, had spent years at sea. Years he had loved. Accomplished as a seaman he jumped ship in the West Indies and worked his way up into acquiring wealth and eventually his own ship. He was a man of resources who had broken the law in foreign seas and lands but had come back to England, wealthy, reformed and in love.

The climb was vertical, requiring strength and agility to reach the shelter at the top. The squire grabbed Bernie's jacket. 'Go straight up, don't try anything, man, or I'll send you down to Davey Jones' locker.'

The man glared at him then, with a lithesome step, he started his ascent. His plan was obviously to outrun the squire and get help at the top. His plan was flawed because Squire Moon was a navy man. He had led his vessel, not from the decks, but had climbed to the crow's nest in order to watch the ocean beneath and the expanse ahead. He was fit and kept up with the lighter man. As Bernie reached the last step, and firm ground, the squire held on to his ankle. As he too climbed up he stared at Bernie's panic stricken face, because one wrong move and the squire could have him plunging to his death on the rocks below. Within moments both men were standing upon the headland behind Marram Hall.

'Now, Bernie, show me where the Shepherds keep the stash, and don't try anything stupid. You will have more need of me if you don't want to swing with them.'

'How can you help me, Squire? You're in gaol for receiving and selling contraband. They ain't going to listen to a character reference from a felon, are they?' Bernie scratched his head through his hat; obviously, nervous and unhappy at the turn of events. 'How did yer escape? Yer an outlaw now.'

'No, they wouldn't, but I'm not an outlaw, man. I'm still in gaol at the moment. Officially, I am, but not actually. So whilst my name is being cleared, you could be murdered and I could prove that I was nowhere near because I'm in the lock up.' He smiled wickedly at the man who was looking less confident with each passing second.

'Why would yer want to kill me?' The man took a step backwards.

The squire caught hold of his arm and spun him around pinning it behind his back and forcing him forward so that his head was leaning over the headland's steep side.

'Who put the contraband in my stables?' He placed the end of the pistol's barrel against Bernie's head. The man sank to his knees. 'Was it the Shepherds?'

'Aye, it was.' He was shaking.

'I warned them to stop their dealings and return to working for their keep, but the man was so lazy. I had no option but to turn them out or hand them over to the revenue. The ba . . . ' He looked down at the trembling figure in front of him. 'Who paid them? Who was it wanted me out of the way and why?' Moon was furious but was struggling to control his voice as he did not want anyone to see or hear him, just yet.

'Mr Cannon, he paid for them. The revenue were getting close to him. They knew that someone had got greedy and was payin' lots to bring in more goods along this coast.' He gasped so Moon shook him hard. 'He wanted you to take the blame then he could . . . ' The man swallowed hard.

'Could what?' Moon asked but he was already forming the full picture in his mind.

'Could have your lass for himself. He'd grown tired of his wife and fancied a youngun' on the side.'

This time it was Squire Moon who swallowed hard because he had so nearly handed her to him so easily. Thank goodness she had been made of a stronger character, like her mother before her.

'Let me go, Squire. I can't tell you anymore, honest.' The man was almost whimpering as if it was sympathy he wanted. However, if it was, then Moon was the wrong person to appeal to.

'One more thing you can tell me before I go and wreak havoc on this vermin; what part in it does the man, Lucas Packman, play?'

14

Lucas did not answer straight away. He appeared to be distracted as he looked at her hand resting in his. The issue of mutual trust regarding her father was one that would have to wait for a resolution. However, Felicity was prepared to, for now.

'You said you wanted to speak to me about two things, Lucas.' She watched closely as his eyes found hers and he smiled warmly. His smile instantly transformed his face from one of serious maturity to that of a young man full of good humour. She wondered if his way of coping with the world was to hide behind a cold façade, yet underneath it there was a young spirited man yearning to be released. Felicity had no doubt as to which side of Lucas would be more fun to live with.

'Yes, Miss Moon, you have affected me deeply. We have both enjoyed a few moments of unrestrained emotions and I feel it is time to speak out about them openly.'

'Are you not being presumptuous, Mr Packman?' she replied, but could not help but grin at him as she spoke.

'No, Felicity, I am being honest. We are more than comfortable in each other's company and with each other's touch.'

Felicity looked out of the window. She felt her cheeks colour as he spoke to her so intimately.

'Do you wish to deny it?' His voice had changed slightly. She saw that he was concerned, apprehensive even, that she may be about to refute his comments or reject him.

'No, Lucas of course not, I would be a fool to even try. Yet, I know so little about you. All this has happened in a relatively short time and without my father's knowledge. Where are you from, Lucas? What of your family?

Where are they? I don't know if I am a pleasant distraction to you, taking you from your work for a few moments, or if what I feel from you in those moments is no more than a passing fancy. Lucas, you are as big a mystery to me as the secret within your store rooms.' She stroked the side of his face with her hand and he kissed her fingers immediately in response.

'I am not used to sharing my personal circumstances with anyone, Felicity. I am a man who is used to being on his own, surrounded by patients and nurses. I can see how much I need to change my habits. I shall learn to share all with you.'

★　★　★

Squire Moon placed the pistol back in his belt and stood Bernie upright. He was shaking from head to foot.

'Calm your nerves, man. I shall see you are all right if you help me now.' He led him to the shelter of the back wall of Marram Hall where they stood for a moment.

'You scared the life from me!' Bernie complained bitterly.

'Do you think you can work for me honestly, man? I will be free soon — exonerated from all this evil and I have wealth that can pay you.' Squire Moon was keeping an eye on a cellar door that was only feet from them.

'Aye, I can, if yer keep that pistol away from me and trained on them that'll wrong you, then, yes.'

'Good, then I want you to wait here and guard the boat. We will need it shortly.' Moon turned his back on him and looked at the cellar door.

'You'd trust me to do that?' Bernie's voice sounded incredulous.

'No, not fully but you can prove yourself now, and then when I visit your mother next time I can tell her she should be proud of her son and, who knows, I may even still forget that she hides things for you in that cottage of hers. Or, I could continue to pay for that crooked leg of hers to be seen to.' He glanced back and could see the look of hurt on Bernie's face. It was good enough, though, because he knew this poor excuse for a man would protect his mother, old witch that she was. They were close. 'You wait here!'

Bernie nodded at him, and the squire entered the cellar knowing the man would still be there when he returned.

★   ★   ★

Felicity leaned back against the stone wall of the window's frame. 'Then share some of your past with me now, Lucas. Let me actually know you.'

He, too, leaned back and folded his arms across his chest as he looked at her. 'I am a man of some wealth,' he began.

'Yes, that I can see.'

'I was not born here.' He glanced out of the window.

'In the north you mean?' Felicity

151

asked, thinking that extracting information from him was a slow painful process.

'No, I mean not from England. I was born in New South Wales. My father was a ship's surgeon and my mother a lady I hardly knew. Circumstances were such that I was brought back to this country by the captain of the ship that my father had served on. My good fortune was that he and I formed a true friendship and he honoured my father's memory by sponsoring me through my schooling and on to qualify as a fully trained surgeon. Whilst he was in the colonies, his wife and daughter perished of cholera back in England. We became as family and I inherited a portion of his estate. So you now know who I am and from whence I came.' He placed his hands on his lap and looked at her. 'Have I satisfied your natural curiosity?'

'What became of your real mother and father?' Felicity asked, seeing his smile drop slightly.

'My father died of fever, and no one

had the knowledge or supplies to save him.' He glanced out of the window.

'And your mother?' she asked quietly.

'Will you marry me, Felicity? No matter who or what our parents are or have been. If I stand by you and your father, could you live here, work here and be happy, as my wife?' He had sat forward and was almost leaning on one knee on the floor as he took both her hands in his.

'Lucas, I have fallen in love with you, you know that. But why not answer my question?' She could see hurt in his eyes and wondered if for a moment she had ruined the most precious of moments.

'Will you not answer mine first? Or does my answer affect yours?'

'Yes, I shall marry you, willingly, but be honest, Lucas. Tell me what it is you hide from?'

He hugged her to him and she felt his breath deepen. When he stood up she could tell his eyes were full of emotion. 'I am a very happy man, Felicity but I will tell you something and you are free to change your mind if you so wish as a result. My mother had been sent out there, transported for stealing food from a market stall in order as not to starve. She was guilty, yet innocent in moral terms. On board ship she slept with my father, he offered her protection and accepted her child. They were never married.' He looked down at her. 'Felicity, I am a bastard and my mother ran away with another man. I don't know what became of her. I only know my father never loved her as I do you, but he was prepared to love his son.' He cleared his throat, 'I ask you again, will you marry me now?'

She stood next to him, held his hands in hers, answering his question with an affirmative kiss.

15

The noise of the door opposite closing made Lucas reluctantly end their embrace. Felicity stepped back and looked at the happy man facing her.

'We shall have to visit Father again. It is important to me that you both can accept one another for what you truly are; for I believe you to be fine people.'

The happiness he showed in his relaxed and open manner was momentarily displaced by a more serious expression, his stance straightening, as if the instinct to recoil into his shell was taking over once more. 'Felicity, would you still accept me if he would not?'

'Lucas, have faith in me if you cannot find it in your heart to trust him also, yet. I have given you my answer but please understand this, he is my father and I want his blessing for us both to be happy together. It is not essential. I will be twenty next spring, but it is my dearest wish that he does not stand in our way and that we may all be reunited. It will make our arrangements so much easier.' She took hold of his hand.

'We . . .' He paused, looking at her thoughtfully. 'I shall do my best to appease his natural doubts about me, but Felicity, he may dismiss me because of my questionable parentage.' He kissed her cheek tenderly and spoke quietly, 'I would do anything for you but this is something I cannot possibly change and I refuse to be ashamed of it.'

'Then, Lucas, let us not burden him with the whole truth. We shall not explain that your father and mother's circumstances were unfortunate. However, we shall say that they died in New South Wales where your father was, like yourself, a surgeon. No more detail will be needed. Talk instead of the man who loved you as his son and who sponsored you. I feel sure that would be adequate to appease him. There is no point in worrying someone over what has gone before, cannot be changed and has no chance of returning to cause you further grief. Is there?'

'You are a resourceful lady. I agree wholeheartedly. Now, I think it is time we explored the mystery that lurks within my store rooms, for you have intrigued me. However, I do not approve of my rooms being used without permission if that indeed is the case. I hope Mrs Shepherd is not letting them out to local villains!' He looked at her wide-eyed, almost playfully, but Felicity did not smile, she saw no jest in his words, for although he thought the idea was preposterous it was exactly what she suspected was the truth.

'What if they are, Lucas? You would be held responsible, if not a party to it and could even end up sharing life with Father in gaol. We need to be cautious, it could be dangerous. Do you have a pistol?' She saw the realisation cross his face that he was possibly harbouring criminals and he had had no idea of it.

'I thought only of my work. I left all the organising of the hall to Mrs Shepherd and Ambrose. I have been blinkered. I presumed they could be trusted.' He walked over to his desk and removed a key from his waistcoat pocket. Unlocking a drawer he removed a pistol and loaded it. 'However, Felicity this is a precautionary measure only. Let's not accuse before we have the evidence.'

'Very wise, for many an innocent man has been arrested and thrown in gaol, I'm sure,' Felicity said directly and he looked at her and nodded. For the first time she saw what she could only presume was doubt cross his face regarding her father, and her heart lifted, filling with hope.

'Felicity you stay here,' he began to tell her but saw her lift up a fire iron and stand by the door.

'I shall do no such thing. We go together for there is safety in numbers and you are not sure that there is a problem here, so we shall find out together, Lucas.' She stared at him.

'Very well, but stay behind me and at the first sign of trouble run.'

She nodded but wondered where she could run to and what of the children. She just prayed there would be no 'trouble'. 'Where did you find Ambrose?'

'Mrs Shepherd hired him from the village. He had lost his boat in a storm and was relieved to find regular work,' Lucas explained.

'And you did not question this further?' Felicity asked, thinking that she had thought it was her who was the gullible and naïve one, yet this worldly man amazed her at his own capacity to be hoodwinked by this Shepherd woman, so centred was he on his work.

He turned the door handle. 'We go quietly,' he answered and led the way to the corridor. He was careful to keep the pistol hidden by his coat.

As she followed Lucas along to the store room Felicity could hear her own heart beat. She was scared and excited at the same time. Soon she would have her answer and she would either look like a complete fanciful fool or their world would become a very dangerous place.

They stopped silently by the door. No sound could be heard from within. He winked at Felicity as he placed his hand on the heavy iron latch. Before lifting it he stopped and examined it. His face lost all jest as he traced the edge of the door with his finger. As he opened the door he showed her that a piece of wood had been added that could lift the latch from inside the room. There was no possible reason for this unless the door was frequently used from both sides, but why? It was a store room. He let the door swing open slowly and she lifted up the lamp so that the light flooded the store room's interior.

'I thought you said that this was too wet to use for a store room?' Felicity asked as she stared at the stone room stacked with old rope of various sizes and weights. There were no bales of illicit silk, brandy, playing cards or bundles of tea. In fact there was no sign of contraband at all. Felicity did not understand. She stared at Lucas who had walked inside the room and was looking around, from one stack to another. Felicity noticed there was a cellar door in the corner.

'Perhaps it is stored down there.' She walked over to the trap door. Lucas knelt down to it. Again there was no dust upon it or debris which indicated to both that it was in regular usage.

'This leads to a cellar which has another door to the outside, facing the headland. Yes, it could be used as an entrance to the hall. I thought it was chained up.' He ran his fingers through his hair. 'I shall find out.' He lifted up the wooden door. There was little light below.

'Take the lamp, Lucas. I shall wait here until you say it is safe, or return to me.' She handed the lamp to him.

'I will only be a moment.' He climbed down the ladder. 'Felicity, there is a clear path that has been used between the outside doors and this room. There is more rope down here too. I shall climb back up. It is time I asked a few questions as to what is happening here.'

Felicity was so busy watching Lucas she had not even glanced back to see if anyone had followed them. As Lucas' face appeared to her once more she saw his eyes look beyond her and knew she was not alone.

'Mrs Shepherd,' he said quite brightly as he ascended the stairs, passing the lamp back to Felicity, who promptly turned to see the woman staring fixedly at them, her arms straight down by her sides. 'What can you tell me about this old rope? What business does it have in my stores?'

Felicity realised he had hidden the pistol by placing his hand in the deep coat pocket but he had still kept it in his hand.

'It's nothing for you to bother about, sir. It's only salvage that the fishermen used but had not managed to store safe like. We didn't think it would cause any problems if it were left 'ere like, until it was needed.' She glanced at Felicity as if she would willingly throttle her. Felicity hoped the sentiment was not lost this time on Lucas, who surely now had had his eyes opened to this woman's deception.

'Why, then, did you not simply ask, and have done with the nonsense of this mysterious behaviour?'

'It seemed such an unimportant matter, sir, next to those that affect the children,' she softened her voice but the eyes were as hard as ever.

Ambrose appeared in the doorway behind her, flustered in appearance and obviously shocked that they were in there. 'What the hell has happened here? Gertrude, what do they know?'

'Hush yer mouth yer blitherin' idiot. They know we are hoarding salvage rope for the village, and Mr Packman ain't that pleased.' She turned to face Ambrose momentarily.

'Oh,' he said as his expression relaxed somewhat.

When they looked back to Lucas he had the pistol trained on Ambrose.

'I can move it if it upsets yer, sir.' Ambrose held his arms in the air. 'I should've checked with you. I was wrong but this isn't needed now is it?'

'You think me stupid, you ungrateful wretch.' He nodded to Felicity. 'Remove his weapons,' he told her. 'This isn't rope. It's filled with tobacco leaves. Cleverly woven, wrapped, oiled and protected. It's a clever ruse, a decoy to throw off the scent from the authorities. I'm harbouring the contraband for a whole network, under my own roof, and no doubt those very villagers who I help are all involved in it.'

16

Ambrose was made to lie face down on the floor. 'What do yer think yer goin' to do, man? Take on the whole village?' Ambrose asked. Mrs Shepherd was still standing as she had when they first saw her.

She suddenly feigned an outburst of emotion and almost threw herself to her knees next to Ambrose. 'Yer can't turn him in, Mr Packman. He's a good man,' she pleaded.

Felicity was surprised at this show of emotion from the icy woman, but as the woman grabbed the hem of Felicity's skirts as she begged pathetically, she soon discovered why. Without warning Felicity found herself pulled into the woman's arms with a knife at her neck.

The fear in Lucas' eyes was only surpassed by what she felt within herself.

Ambrose got to his feet.

'Aye, it is a fine to do, this. Now, you listen to Ambrose, Mr Packman. I'll have yer gun if yer please or the lassie'll suffer.'

Lucas lowered the pistol. Felicity tried to struggle free and was rewarded with a nick by the knife on her throat for her troubles. She let out a small gasp and Lucas instantly gave up the gun. What a mess they were in. Felicity could not believe their folly and ill luck.

Ambrose pointed the pistol at Lucas and told him to descend the stairs. He was followed down by Ambrose, who kept cautiously out of arm's reach. Lucas' face was flushed with anger as he saw Mrs Shepherd manhandle Felicity until she almost fell to the floor as they, too, joined them in the cellar.

'What do you intend to do with us?' Felicity asked, as Mrs Shepherd roughly pushed her forward towards the outer door.

'You'll find out sooner than you want to know, but let's say you two sweeties went for one walk too many on the headland, eh.' The woman sniggered and Felicity took Lucas' outstretched hand. The look they exchanged she would remember for ever, however long or short that was to be, for it was filled with heartrending love and loss, as if time and motion had stopped around them. The moment broke in a timely and shattering sound as the echo of a pistol shot rang out and mingled with the piercing scream of Mrs Shepherd as Ambrose fell into a bloody heap on the stony floor beside her. This time, when the woman bent double, her sobs were genuine.

Felicity and Lucas stared incredulously as the figure in the shadows stepped forward to reveal her father's face.

'You killed him!' Lucas said as he checked the man's pulse, removing the pistol and restraining Mrs Shepherd's hands that had tried to claw at his face like a wild animal.

'He's already dead. This is Ambrose

Shepherd, the man who I believe you thought I had already killed. They were given fair warning not to use my cottages for this trade.' He kicked one of the coils of tobacco rope. 'But they wouldn't and even plotted my downfall with the help of Cannon to have me arrested as the money behind the ring. They'd have done the same to you if he'd ordered it so.'

'What do we do now, Father? How did you escape?' Felicity ran to him and hugged him, her mind full of fear for the mess they were all in.

'We return Mr Cannon's goods to him and inform the authorities where he hides them. This time the right man will end up in the gaol. First, though, we dispose of Ambrose as . . . '

'You see to the tobacco, I am a surgeon, I shall deal with the body. This woman will return with her tobacco.'

'Like hell I will.' She struggled to fight, but Lucas held her firmly.

'Felicity, go to the store and retrieve the laudanum, she is distressed.'

Felictity did. When she returned to them there was another man helping to move some of the ropes outside.

Soon Mrs Shepherd was fast asleep, not one of peace, knowing she would wake up in gaol as a drunken lost wretch. The last words Lucas spoke to her as she drifted off was that New South Wales was the best place for her sort — they needed strong women.

It took Lucas, the squire and Bernie all their strength to lower enough of the rope to the boat to ensure that they had evidence to put Cannon away for a long stretch. Then it was time for Squire Moon to descend with Bernie back to the boat. He had to return to the gaol, as if nothing had happened, and await his official release.

As Bernie climbed onto the ladder, Lucas turned to him and said, 'I saw you last month at the cemetery. Your mother, wasn't it?'

Bernie nodded and looked at Squire Moon.

'Your mother was already dead?' he

asked, obviously surprised.

Bernie nodded again.

'I'm sorry, lad.' Then he added, 'Your loyalty will be rewarded.' Bernie half smiled and then disappeared from sight.

Next, Squire Moon climbed over. 'Look after my girl, Packman. We'll talk about your future when you visit and I know I still have one.'

Lucas nodded, and as Felicity stepped forward, still holding Lucas' hand, her father looked at her. 'I have to go, lass, but look after this man. There are few good ones about. You've been lucky, lass, now be off with you.'

Her father also disappeared from her sight and Lucas wrapped a strong arm around her.

'Felicity, I have much to do. Stay with the children. I have to destroy the rest of the 'ropes', remove Mrs Shepherd and her ill-gotten goods, then see to Ambrose.'

'Father murdered him,' she whispered in a shaky breath.

'He saved our lives, and you cannot kill a dead man. Besides, your father is in gaol, an innocent man.'

He kissed her, and briefly held her to him.

Later, she saw from Hannah's window James and Lucas take the wagon out, and closed the curtain. Hannah's eyes opened. Felicity sat on the bed and stroked the child's hair. She looked frightened. 'It's all right, Hannah, the pirates have all gone now.'

Hannah opened her eyes once more and smiled before falling back into a contented sleep.

Felicity lost track of the hours that passed by before the wagon returned. All she knew was that day had dawned. She wrapped up in her warmest cloak and stood outside, watching the sea and waiting to hear the wheels of the wagon turning. Eventually, the gentle noise was carried to her ears by the wind, and she saw it approaching. Numbed by all that had happened, she ran to Lucas. He handed the reins to James and jumped down to her. Wrapping his arms around her he swung her off her feet.

'I was so worried about you.' She kissed him and he her.

'I had a lot to do but all will be well. Come and meet our new member of staff.' He took her by the hand to the back of the wagon.

Felicity's smile grew as there with her bags and belongings was the familiar face of the woman who had sent her to Lucas and changed her life forever. 'Edna!' Felicity exclaimed and hugged the woman to her.

'Calm down, dear. You really need to control that emotional nature of yours. I could really do with a dish of tea.'

Lucas climbed back up next to James and Felicity sat next to Edna as they returned to the hall.

'I knew you were right for each other,' Edna whispered to her as the wagon moved along.

'Thank you, Edna,' Felicity said warmly to her, and stared at her friend's face. 'My father is innocent, you know.'

'Yes, dear, I've always known, but it took someone in Lucas' position to help you to prove it.'

Felicity glanced up at him. He looked tired and stressed but today they would be able to put the past behind them, and with trust and honesty, look forward to their own future together.

THE END

We do hope that you have enjoyed reading this large print book.

Did you know that all of our titles are available for purchase?

We publish a wide range of high quality large print books including:
Romances, Mysteries, Classics General Fiction Non Fiction and Westerns

Special interest titles available in large print are:
The Little Oxford Dictionary Music Book, Song Book Hymn Book, Service Book

Also available from us courtesy of Oxford University Press:
Young Readers' Dictionary (large print edition) Young Readers' Thesaurus (large print edition)

For further information or a free brochure, please contact us at:
**Ulverscroft Large Print Books Ltd., The Green, Bradgate Road, Anstey, Leicester, LE7 7FU, England.
Tel:** (00 44) **0116 236 4325
Fax:** (00 44) **0116 234 0205**

Other titles in the
Linford Romance Library:

A HEART DIVIDED

Sheila Holroyd

Life is hard for Anne and her father under Cromwell's harsh rule, which has reduced them from wealth to poverty. When tragedy strikes it looks as if there is no one she can turn to for help. With one friend fearing for his life and another apparently lost to her, a man she hates sees her as a way of fulfilling all his ambitions. Will she have to surrender to him or lose everything?

SAFE HARBOUR

Cara Cooper

When Adam Hawthorne with his sharp suit and devastating looks drives into the town of Seaport, Cassandra knows he's dangerous. Not only do his plans threaten to ruin her successful harbourside restaurant, but also Adam stirs painful memories she'd rather forget. When Cassandra's sister Ellie turns up, in trouble as usual, Cassandra needs all her considerable strength to cope. But will discovering dark secrets from Adam's past change Cassandra's future? And will he be her saviour or her downfall?

THE HAPPY HOSTAGE

Charles Stuart

When an agreement is made with the U.S.A. to build missile bases in Carmania, Elisabeth Renner and her friends plot to kidnap the American ambassador to Carmania and force the agreement to be cancelled. However, they get the wrong man: Charles Gresham, a budding British business tycoon. And he soon finds himself sympathising with his pretty captor. Then Elisabeth reluctantly decides to call it all off, and things really go wrong — when Charles doesn't want to be released!

STILL THE ONE

Joan Reeves

Ally Fletcher fights her way through a torrential downpour to Mr Burke Winslow and his bride at their marriage ceremony! Ally's arrival at the church halts the nuptials when she delivers her bombshell: the groom is already married — to her! However, this businessman isn't in love: he needs a wife for two weeks, purely for financial reasons. Anyone will do — even his insufferable ex. Soon Burke and Ally are temporarily reliving their disastrous marriage — and their sensational, sizzling honeymoon . . .